Goshen County Library
P9-EEB-911
2001 East "A" Street
Torrington, WY 82240

3-0.5			c. B.
BA			
Gdewph			

Family Ties

This Large Print Book carries the
Seal of Approval of N.A.V.H.

Family Ties

Bonnie K. Winn

Goshen County Library
2001 East "A" Street
Torrington, WY 82240
83-109

Thorndike Press • Waterville, Maine

Copyright © 2002 by Bonnie K. Winn

All rights reserved.

All characters in this book have no existence outside the imagination of the author and have no relation whatsoever to anyone
bearing the same name or names. They are not even
distantly inspired by any individual known or unknown to the
author, and all incidents are pure invention.

Published in 2005 by arrangement with Harlequin Books S.A.

Thorndike Press® Large Print Christian Romance.

The tree indicium is a trademark of Thorndike Press.

The text of this Large Print edition is unabridged.
Other aspects of the book may vary from the original edition.

Set in 16 pt. Plantin by Al Chase.

Printed in the United States on permanent paper.

Library of Congress Cataloging-in-Publication Data
Winn, Bonnie K.
    Family ties / by Bonnie K. Winn.
        p. cm. — (Thorndike Press large print Christian romance)
    ISBN 0-7862-7243-0 (lg. print : hc : alk. paper)
        1. Widowers — Fiction.   2. Single fathers — Fiction.
    3. Church membership — Fiction.   4. Sisters — Death —
    Fiction.   5. Triplets — Fiction.   6. Texas — Fiction.
    7. Large type books.   I. Title.   II. Thorndike Press large
    print Christian romance series.
    PS3573.I532257 F36
        813'.54—dc22   2004024169

Dedicated to my husband, Howard,
a man of faith *and* romance,
an irresistible combination.

National Association for Visually Handicapped
serving the partially seeing

As the Founder/CEO of NAVH, the only national health agency solely devoted to those who, although not totally blind, have an eye disease which could lead to serious visual impairment, I am pleased to recognize Thorndike Press★ as one of the leading publishers in the large print field.

Founded in 1954 in San Francisco to prepare large print textbooks for partially seeing children, NAVH became the pioneer and standard setting agency in the preparation of large type.

Today, those publishers who meet our standards carry the prestigious "Seal of Approval" indicating high quality large print. We are delighted that Thorndike Press is one of the publishers whose titles meet these standards. We are also pleased to recognize the significant contribution Thorndike Press is making in this important and growing field.

Lorraine H. Marchi, L.H.D.
Founder/CEO
NAVH

★ Thorndike Press encompasses the following imprints: Thorndike, Wheeler, Walker and Large Print Press.

To every thing there is a season and a time
for every event under heaven . . .
a time to weep and a time to laugh,
a time to mourn and a time to dance . . .
a time to embrace . . . and a time to love.
— *Ecclesiastes* 3: 1–8

Prologue

†

Houston, Texas

The day was too bright, the sun too cheerful, Cindy Thompson decided. It should be gray, overcast, perhaps drenched with rain or swept by relentless wind. But only a mild breeze stirred the sweet, spring air. It was the best time of year in Houston. Plagued by heat and humidity, the near-coastal city could rarely boast of mild, pleasant days. But it was something Cindy had been accustomed to, growing up there alongside her sister, Julia.

But Julia no longer had to worry about hot and cold, about sunshine and rain. Still the light shone mercilessly on her mahogany coffin, revealing the grain of the highly polished wood and the creamy hue of the pure white floral spray. Two lone ivory ribbons proclaimed "wife" and "mother."

Cindy swallowed another rush of tears, her gaze sliding yet again to her brother-in-law, Flynn Mallory, and his three tiny, identical daughters. Julia would be pleased,

Cindy thought irrationally. The girls were dressed beautifully. Matching dresses of deep green velvet, no doubt from Houston's finest children's store, shiny black Mary Janes, spotless ivory tights.

The triplets were just barely twenty-two months old, matching bundles of endless energy. Cindy wondered how Flynn had managed to ready them with such precision. From what she'd known, Julia had been their sole caretaker since Flynn was always working, striving to improve his already-prosperous business.

Cindy had offered to help with the girls, but Flynn had firmly refused. Not much had changed. Flynn was still holding her at arm's length. Shaking away the painful memories, Cindy bent her head for the closing prayer, offering one of her own for her beloved sister.

Silence sliced over the crowd now as they waited for Flynn to rise. He did so slowly, trying to hold three tiny hands with his own larger ones. Taking that cue, Cindy reached for baby Alice's hand, since she was seated beside her. Flynn didn't protest, for once looking out of control and a bit lost.

"Mommy?" little Beth asked, looking as lost as her father.

Flynn's face worked, his lips seemingly

trying to form words his heart refused to utter.

Seeing his pain, Cindy knelt down beside the girls, enveloping them in a hug. Then she gave each of them a single pink rosebud, Julia's favorite. Quietly she led them to the casket, allowing each to place a flower on the sun-warmed wood.

Flynn watched helplessly, barely acknowledging soft-spoken condolences of friends as they filed past. Clearly his world had been shattered. Julia had been a rock, the nucleus of their family. Cindy had always imagined her sister growing old, surrounded by Flynn and a passel of adoring grandchildren. But that wasn't to be.

Any more than her own happiness was to be.

Cindy shook away the thought, immediately ashamed of her pettiness. Her only concern could be the children. Cindy intended to delay her return to Rosewood. She wouldn't abandon her sister's children. She owed it to Julia and even Flynn's resistance wouldn't stop her. She knew, however, it was only temporary. She couldn't hope to be included where she wasn't wanted. But in the meantime she would shower the girls with love . . . and pray they wouldn't forget her.

Chapter One

†

Rosewood, Texas
One year later

Driving slowly, Flynn Mallory surveyed the main street of the small Hill Country town he'd chosen to call home, a hamlet far different from Houston. And incredibly far from the only roots he'd ever known. He and Julia had never visited Rosewood. Cindy had made the infrequent trips to Houston, saying she could combine business with pleasure. It had suited Flynn. It wasn't easy to travel with the triplets and he'd felt no need to survey Rosewood until now.

But Rosewood offered what his daughters really wanted — their aunt Cindy. For the millionth time, Flynn regretted the loss of his family . . . his entire family. There was no loving family member to turn to. No one who could offer help or advice. No Mallory grandparent, aunt or uncle who could help the girls know they were loved. Cindy wouldn't have been his choice if he'd had anyone else to turn to. But his relatives were all dead and Cindy was the only member left of Julia's family. Cindy was irresponsible and fun loving, but he could provide the stability his children needed. They could visit with Cindy once a week and get the emotional bonding they craved while he ensured a secure environment.

For a moment Flynn thought he'd taken a wrong turn. The eclectic, charming neighborhood was old and well-worn, the yards filled with ancient oaks and carefully pruned rose gardens.

Expecting a sleekly modern condo, Flynn looked for a place where he could turn his vehicle around. But then he spotted Cindy's address. There was no mistake. The numbers sat atop a nameplate of swirling letters that spelled out Thompson. But he still wasn't reassured. The softly faded old Victorian house didn't fit his image of Cindy.

Climbing out of his SUV, Flynn strolled up the red brick sidewalk. A magnificent aged magnolia tree perfumed the air, its dark glossy leaves looking as though they'd been polished by hand. Flynn knew the slow-growing tree had to be at least one hundred years old. But the house looked that and then some.

Unable to stop staring, he climbed the steps to the wraparound porch. Flynn reached for a doorbell and found an old brass knocker instead. He glanced upward at the gently curving eaves, pounding a bit more loudly than he intended. And within seconds the door whipped open. A disheveled, startled-looking Cindy stared at him.

Since she looked flustered, he offered a smile. "I *did* call."

Cindy pushed at a lock of flame-colored hair framing her forehead. Then she pulled back the door, opening it wider, looking surprisingly flushed. "Of course. I'm sorry. I got caught up in some painting and lost track of time." She held up a brush covered in bright yellow paint, then glanced down at her paint-splattered overalls. "Give me just a minute to wash my hands." She gestured past the foyer to an inviting room. "Make yourself comfortable."

Not surprised that the irresponsible Cindy was off schedule, Flynn nodded, walked in, then went down the single wooden step into the parlor.

It was the only word to describe the room. A huge, leaded-glass bay window kept the old-fashioned room bright. The whimsical furniture was as intriguing as it was impractical. Delicate needlepoint chairs that didn't look as though they could support real humans were drawn up to a table set with

14

translucent cups and saucers, a matching bone-china teapot, and bite-size sandwiches.

Raising his eyebrows, he noted that a fainting couch replaced a more conventional sofa. Nothing about Cindy's house met his expectations.

"I'm sorry," she said, gliding into the room, sounding a bit breathless. "I promised my friend Katherine I'd have the bookcases for the Sunday school rooms painted this week. There didn't seem to be so many when I volunteered," she ended with a smile.

He shrugged, knowing little about Sunday school and its expectations. He'd been a boy when he'd last attended church. And that was a lifetime ago.

She moved toward the prepared table with a teapot. "It's hot." She gestured to the thick fabric covering the pot. "The cozy keeps it warm. Tea?"

"It's not necessary."

Cindy kept her smile in place. "Perhaps not, but it's very civil."

He relented, realizing she was being gracious and he was being ungrateful. There had been little time in the last year for niceties. Every available moment had been spent chasing the triplets and trying to decide whether he was making the right decision in moving to Rosewood. It wasn't Cindy's fault that he was feeling so pressed. She was simply trying to help. He forced himself to relax. "My appointment with the Realtor isn't for another hour."

Cindy poured the tea and handed Flynn a cup. "So you're still certain you want to move here?"

Awkwardly he balanced the small, fragile cup, not ready to admit his apprehension. "I'm ready for a change of scenery. Everywhere I look or go, I'm reminded of Julia." He caught her questioning gaze. "Not that I don't want to remember . . ."

"I understand. But won't you have to face it sometime?"

He frowned. "I've faced her death, the fact that I have to go on alone. But the girls need a change." Unwilling to share how upsetting this was with her, he switched subjects. "And I couldn't take looking for another baby-sitter."

She offered him the sandwich platter. "That bad?"

He took a few of the crustless diamond-shaped snacks, his hands seeming unusually large and clumsy amidst the fragile delicacies. "Worse. I wanted to be sure that whoever was taking care of the girls was responsible."

She drew her brows together, a shadow eclipsing the bright curiosity in her eyes. "That didn't work?"

He paused for a moment, examining the odd little sprouts that edged the filling of the delicate sandwich. "Depends on your point of view. The first baby-sitter, Mrs. Sanders, took charge immediately. I imagine there were POW camps run with more humor. Even I was tiptoeing around the woman. I didn't want the girls growing up believing they had to snap to attention in their own home."

Cindy laughed. "Surely there was a compromise."

"I hired former schoolteachers, and even a registered nurse."

"Weren't they better than the commandant?"

"Somewhat. But the truth is no professional care-taker's going to love the girls and care for them like someone in the family would."

Cindy's fingers tightened around the handle of her teacup and she paused for a moment before she spoke. "You're right, of course. But aren't you worried about uprooting the girls?"

"From preschool?" Flynn shook his head, knowing it wasn't the girls who would be uprooted. "They're young enough to adjust to a move. More so than to the loss of their mother. The only reason I'm considering relocating is because of them." Even if it meant reconnecting with a woman he considered best forgotten. "Everything I do is in their best interest."

"I know it is, Flynn," she responded, her gaze resting on him intently. "I'm just trying to be a good sounding board. This is a big step, and Julia's only been gone for a year."

"True. But I didn't just wake up one morning with a wild hair. I'm able to provide almost every monetary need my children have, but I can't produce a family I don't have."

Cindy nodded, knowing he, too, was the last member of his family. "I may be one of the few people in the world who can understand that." It had been a devastating blow for Cindy to lose Julia since they were the last two left in their family. Still, something about Flynn's uncharacteristic behavior bothered her. He was not the sort of man who moved to an unseen town on a whim.

"And you can't force a connection," Flynn was saying. "Children either feel that for a person, or they don't. And the girls feel it with you."

Tears misted in Cindy's eyes and her lips

18

trembled, emotion overshadowing caution. "They mean so much to me. Thank you for showing your trust in me."

Flynn hesitated, but knew he had to be honest. His daughters were too precious to him for anything less than the truth. "You won't have to take on any responsibility with them."

She blanched, then recovered quickly. "Of course."

Flynn didn't want to hurt her, but she had to know the real purpose of their move, why he was doing this against all reason. "The girls need an emotional connection with you, rather than help with their up-bringing."

Cindy's head bobbed up and down a bit too vigorously. "I understand. And I suppose you've worked out something for your company."

He tried not to remember how much that hurt, as well. "After Julia died, my vice presidents banded together, running things so efficiently that it became apparent I wasn't needed for the day-to-day operations."

"Won't you miss it?" she asked softly. "It's been a big part of your life."

More than she could possibly know. "I'm not content to glide along on past accomplishments." He forced enthusiasm into his voice, guessing otherwise the words would ring with empty truth. "I need something new, something challenging."

"And you can find that in Rosewood?" Cindy asked skeptically.

Flynn managed a reasonable chuckle. "Aren't you being a bit snobbish about your adopted home?"

"Not at all. Just realistic. We're a long way from boardrooms and stock quotes."

"Not as far as you think. With the Internet, you can be in Iceland and have as much access to Wall Street as anyone in New York. But I just want the right place to retreat, one where I can recoup, try to start again."

Her expression softened. "I know it's been difficult for you. I miss Julia terribly every day. I remember her laugh, her way of making the worst situation bearable." Cindy met his eyes. "It must be far worse for you — especially trying to be mother and father to the girls. But the important thing is that the girls *do* have you. The rest will come in time."

Uncharacteristic doubt assailed him as it had since Julia had died. "You're so sure?"

Cindy took a deep breath, the green of her eyes deepening to near emerald. He wondered at the emotion that skittered across her face. "As sure as any one person can be. The Lord never gives us burdens that are heavier than we can bear."

He shrugged impatiently, thinking her talk of faith must be her latest fad, one that would no doubt be forgotten soon. He knew from experience that she'd be better off without that treacherous fantasy. "Church seems like ancient history."

She searched his eyes. "That's too bad. You won't find anything more relevant and timely."

He glanced at his watch. "Speaking of time, would you like to go with me to meet the Realtor? After all, you recommended Linda Baker. Besides, you know the town. You can steer me away from any lemons."

The edge of her mouth curled upward. "Kind of takes the adventure out of the process, doesn't it?"

"You've forgotten, Cindy. I don't care for adventure."

Cindy hadn't forgotten. She'd simply pushed that truth to the back of her consciousness. Along with the cache of emotions Flynn Mallory created. While he waited in her parlor, Cindy reached for a change of clothes, remembering the first time she'd met him.

She and Julia were at a party. Spotting

Flynn Mallory, Cindy knew immediately that everything about him seemed larger than life. From his shock of unruly chestnut hair to the fire in his dark eyes, to the fierceness of his determination. She had never met anyone like him. Immediately she was attracted to his strength and purpose. Unlike the other young men in the group, he had a maturity and confidence that set him apart. Cindy hadn't doubted from the moment she met him that he would succeed. Everything about him said he wouldn't allow anything less.

She'd been equally determined to make him hers.

And that remained one of the foremost failures in her life.

After she and Flynn had shared one electrifying gaze that she still couldn't forget, Cindy had fallen hard and fast. Unable to still what had momentarily flowed between them, in the ensuing weeks Cindy had employed every trick she knew to interest him. Not because she wanted a mild flirtation, but because she had truly fallen in love with him.

But the more bizarre and outlandish her efforts, the more he withdrew. She and Julia saw him often in their social circle. But Flynn began to concentrate on Julia. He clearly valued Julia's stability and desire to have a family.

And despite his initial attraction to Cindy, he seemed determined to ignore the adventure she craved. And that was something she'd never understood. For it seemed the fire in his eyes matched hers. It was the first and only time she'd ever felt that way about a man.

Even though it broke her heart, she backed off when he and Julia became serious. And she steadfastly accepted the position of maid of honor for Julia, cheerfully organizing showers, parties and wedding breakfasts.

If there were tears beneath the smiles, no one knew. And Cindy told herself that her feelings for Flynn would fade. That in time, she would come to view him as a brother. But that hadn't happened.

Instead, to extricate herself from the situation, a few months after the wedding she had moved to Rosewood where her best friend, Katherine Blake Carlson, was the pastor of the community church.

In the time that followed, Cindy had seen her sister far less frequently than she would have liked. She made sure she visited when Flynn was away on business, keeping the pain at bay. When she did occasionally run into him, it all rushed back, though. He was unfailingly polite when they met, but she could tell that despite the passage of time he still saw her as flighty, unfocused. And she didn't try to change that opinion. It didn't really matter anymore.

Yet his tie to Julia and subsequent place in their family remained an unhealed wound. So Rosewood became Cindy's escape, her place of peace.

And now Flynn Mallory was shattering that to bits.

Cindy shook back her hair, added earrings, then picked up her purse, feeling strangely nervous about being in Flynn's company.

For an instant she remembered his startling phone call a month earlier — the one that promised to change her life and threaten her secure existence. She'd wanted nothing more than to ask him to stay away — not to move to Rosewood. But she couldn't deny her nieces a chance for happiness. If she truly could help them, she wouldn't put her own concerns ahead of theirs.

And it was nothing short of a miracle that Flynn had asked for her help. It was a complete turnaround for him . . . and a point she couldn't stop questioning. Why, *why* was he doing this?

Taking a breath, Cindy stepped through the expansive arched doorway that led into the parlor. Flynn turned just then. And despite her best intentions, she caught her breath.

He stepped forward and she exhaled, praying silently for strength.

"I'm ready," she announced, forcing cheerfulness into her tone.

When he glanced at her, she wondered if it was disapproval she saw registering in his expression. Self-consciously, she smoothed the soft fabric of her long, flowing, deep purple skirt. Belatedly it occurred to her that the choice might be a bit wild for Flynn. Julia had always dressed and acted much more conservatively. Their parents' death had stolen Julia's sense of adventure. Cindy had reacted in just the opposite fashion — she needed excitement and new challenges to feel alive. But then everything about her had been too wild for Flynn.

She tried not to dwell on that as they walked outside and settled into his SUV. Once inside it, however, her nervousness increased. The spacious vehicle seemed oddly intimate.

"So, what do you think of Rosewood?" she asked, trying to chase away her nerves.

He shrugged as he handed her the directions Linda had given him. "Haven't seen much of it yet."

"There's a lot of history here, but not anything too high-tech."

"You have electricity and phone lines?"

She blinked. "Of course." Then she realized he was teasing. "Except on candle day, of course."

He took his attention from the road. "Candle day?"

She met his gaze. "Keeps us from becoming too dependent on technology."

He lifted his brows in acknowledgment. "Guess you hope it doesn't fall on stormy days, then."

She pursed her lips. "So the wind doesn't blow out our candles?"

"Right."

The teasing exchange allowed her to relax a fraction. "It's really a good place to raise children. People watch out for each other, the schools are filled with teachers who care. And our church pulls together through good times and bad."

"You make it sound idyllic."

Cindy turned to gaze at the crepe myrtle trees in full bloom, their delicate blossoms coloring the landscape. As she did, she thought of her own loneliness, the empty nights, the longing for what would never be.

"Not exactly idyllic. But genuine."

"That's rare enough in the world today."

Agreeing, Cindy nodded. Seeing that they were nearing the turn to the address he'd given her, she pointed out the way.

"Linda promised to show me the best Rosewood has to offer," Flynn commented as he made another turn.

"She's a great Realtor, as well as a nice person," Cindy acknowledged. "And hopefully she'll have some decent listings."

Glancing at her, he frowned. "That was said with a bit of doubt."

Cindy hesitated. "Rosewood doesn't have much growth, so there's not a lot of new home construction. People tend to settle in and stay in one place. I think only one new subdivision's been built in the last twenty years. So, not much was available when I started looking. Luckily I was able to stay with Katherine because it took me a while to find my place."

"Is that how you wound up in the Victorian?"

"Oh, no! It's exactly what I wanted. That's why it took so long. I've dreamed of owning one of the painted ladies as long as I can remember. I didn't want to settle for anything else." Or *anyone* else, she added silently.

Flynn glanced at her in baffled astonishment and she wondered why he seemed so surprised. Belatedly she also wondered just what he *had* expected.

Then, rounding the corner, they arrived at the first house. A cheerful Linda Baker waited on the front porch.

As they walked through the house, Cindy found her gaze going more toward Flynn than the smallish interior. Sunshine spilled through the uncurtained windows, brightening the rooms. Flynn turned just then and the light framed his uncompromising features. Despite the fact that his lips didn't rest in a smile, she was so drawn to him, it was nearly a physical ache. What was it about this one man that touched her heart in a way no other had?

His gaze shifted, meeting hers, and for a moment she glimpsed uncertainty. As instantly she knew it to be a rarity for him. Again she wondered why he was doing this. How could he consider moving to this sleepy town so far from everything that was intrinsically him?

Flynn again shifted his gaze, obviously unwilling to share that truth with her. But it didn't stop her wondering, nor her awareness when he brushed by.

She pulled back swiftly, yet she could see

his eyes widen in startled surprise. Her vivid purple skirt twirling, she spun away from him, practically running toward the front door.

A few moments later Linda joined her, keeping her voice low. "I really thought he'd like this one."

Perhaps if Flynn didn't find a house to his liking, he would abandon his plan to move to Rosewood, Cindy mused silently. Just as instantly she remembered her bond with Julia, her responsibility to her sister's children.

Soon they were on the way to the second house. Then the third. Again, Flynn patiently outlined all of his needs to Linda, who listened carefully, but not too hopefully.

And it was only downhill from there. Everything they'd seen was in need of major repair. Also, none of the houses seemed to suit Flynn. Even with significant renovations, Cindy couldn't see him in any of these homes, including the one they now viewed.

"This one's a bit on the modern side," Linda told him, obviously trying to interject some enthusiasm into her voice for the not-too-inviting house. "That should appeal to a forward-thinking man."

"Hmm," Flynn replied.

"It has quite a bit of potential," Linda added hopefully.

Flynn glanced at the unusual roofline. "What was this originally? A school?"

"Yes. But it had extensive renovations when it was converted. The kitchen —"

Flynn, however, was shaking his head. "Anything left to show me?"

"I'm afraid not. The only other listings in town are a few two-bedroom starter homes that aren't nearly as large as you've told me you need. Honestly, if I thought another Realtor would have something more appropriate, I would tell you. But there's only one other company in town and we're both on a multi-listing system. I'm afraid that with this temporary housing shortage, there just isn't much of a selection." Linda drew her brows together. "Actually, knowing what you want, especially considering your preference for contemporary, I think you ought to consider building."

"Won't that take a while?" Cindy asked, wondering if this could be the relief she'd hoped for.

"Probably," Linda agreed.

"But I've already sold my house in Houston," Flynn told them in a surprisingly defeated tone.

Cindy tried not to let her breath escape in

a huge whoosh. "You did?"

"Yep. I thought I'd find something here."

"Perhaps Linda has the right idea — build a house. Can't you hold off the closing date on your house?"

"Nope." His expression tightened. "We closed last Friday."

Cindy winced.

"I wish I hadn't told the girls we were moving right away," Flynn muttered. "I realize now it was a hasty plan, but I never thought I'd encounter a housing shortage."

Linda brightened suddenly. "Cindy, you've got a ton of room at your house. If Flynn decides to build, maybe he and his kids could stay with you until his house is finished."

Nonplussed, Cindy stared first at Linda, than at Flynn.

"We couldn't impose," Flynn began.

"Well, it wouldn't be imposing," Cindy found herself saying. What could she say with Linda staring at her with those puppy-dog eyes and Flynn looking like a stalwart, if bereft, widower? "It can't take that long to build a house," she added weakly.

"And I have the perfect contractor!" Linda exclaimed. "Roy Johnson — my cousin. He just finished a job, and I know he's available. And there's plenty of land for sale locally."

Flynn still looked torn. His gaze was probing as he met Cindy's. "Are you sure about this?"

Her throat thickened as every bit of her common sense screamed *No!* "Of course. What's family for?"

"But this is a lot to ask," he responded in a tone that made Cindy wonder if he wanted to be talked out of the plan.

"Cindy's always helping everybody in town!" Linda exclaimed. "I'm sure she'd love to help her own family for a change. She told me about those darling triplets of yours."

Cindy stared helplessly at Flynn, realizing she'd been caught in a trap of her own good works and inability to spit out the truth.

But he was looking more than a bit flummoxed and reluctant himself. "I can rent an apartment while the house is being built."

Linda shook her head. "Not in this town. Everything for rent is snapped up by the oil folks — Adair Petroleum's opened a new regional office here to oversee pipeline and trucking operations. The only housing you can find is for sale. And there aren't a lot of those — well, you just saw them. Because of this small boom, there's a real housing shortage. To be honest, it probably won't last long. Everyone at Adair should be settled in a few months down the road and then things will get back to normal. But that won't do you a lot of good right now."

Flynn looked at the unattractive house. "Then I'll buy something temporary."

"That's ridiculous," Cindy burst out. "Everything we've seen today will take a lot of fixing up just to be livable. By that time, your house could be built." She felt herself digging an even deeper hole, but knew her conscience wouldn't allow her to be quiet. The triplets didn't deserve more disappointment. At their age, a few months' delay would seem like an eternity. "Linda's right. I have plenty of room. You and the girls can stay with me."

"I would like to oversee the construction of the house," Flynn pondered, still not sounding convinced, but rather, trapped.

Which put them both in the same position.

"Then it's all settled!" Linda exclaimed, looking like a Girl Scout who'd done a good deed, and certainly the only happy member of their trio. "I'll assemble lists of available land right away."

Cindy forced her smile to widen as she met Flynn's gaze. "Looks like you're all set."

He considered her words for a moment,

looking as though he wished he had another option. Any other option. "I can put the furniture in storage. We could probably be here in about two weeks. That'll give you time to change your mind, Cindy."

Two weeks. The words flashed through her like a bad mantra. Two weeks until everything she knew was turned upside down. Two weeks until the man she loved moved into her life. And her house.

Chapter Two

†

Flynn couldn't hold three hands at once. He tried, but one always slipped away. He'd taught the girls to hold each other's hands so they wouldn't get separated. But on days like today excitement outweighed caution.

They stood on the curving sidewalk that led to Cindy's house. As they did, Flynn took a deep breath, wondering yet again if moving to Rosewood was a mistake. He'd almost turned the SUV back around a dozen times on the drive from Houston. It didn't matter that the house was sold; he could find another place to live in Houston.

"Swing!" Alice exclaimed just then, pointing to the old-fashioned two-seater that was suspended from the tall rafters on the front porch.

"An' flowers," the softer-spoken Mandy added.

"Mommy flowers," Beth chimed in, referring to the roses her mother had loved.

Flynn felt that subtle clutching of his heart — one that always followed mention of Julia. The girls spoke of her less and less often, their young memories fading already. Yet, each comment was a new wound. However, it was a wound of guilt — one that came from the reminder that he wasn't thinking enough of Julia.

Flynn was appalled that he, too, was beginning to forget little things, that days passed with little or no thought of her. He wondered if the progression was normal, or if he was as unfeeling as his own mother had been.

The front door opened just then and Cindy stepped onto the porch.

"Cinny!" In unison, the girls shouted their name for her. Breaking away from him, they hurried up the sidewalk and then the wide steps. Reaching the porch, three compact bodies hurtled toward his sister-in-law.

Laughing, she caught them, exchanging huge hugs and kisses. "Hello, darlings! I thought you'd *never* get here!"

"Us here," Beth replied, grinning.

"And you're so tall," Cindy continued. She cocked her head, studying them in mock amazement. "By next week you'll all be as tall as me!"

The girls giggled madly.

"Uh-uh!" Alice protested.

"I don't know," Cindy teased, shaking

her head. Then she reached down, picking up the toddler.

Immediately, the other two clambered to be picked up, as well. Still laughing, Cindy scooted over to the swing, reaching for the other two, lifting them up to sit beside her.

"Now *there's* a picture," Flynn told her as he neared the porch, realizing as he spoke it was true. Cindy looked as unaffected and natural as the triplets. It was a warm and fuzzy image that could have graced a magazine layout.

"Daddy sit, too!" Beth demanded.

But he shook his head as he bent automatically to kiss Cindy's cheek.

The startled response in Cindy's eyes surprised him. But then it seemed to surprise her, as well.

Cindy spoke quickly to fill the gap. "Why don't we go inside and get you all settled in?"

"Swing!" Beth demanded when Cindy stood up.

Flynn plucked his daughter from the swing, preempting her demand. The more malleable Mandy moved toward the door without protest. Alice, somewhere between mild Mandy and belligerent Beth, seemed to realize it was best to comply, as well.

"Why don't I show you where the bedrooms are?" Cindy told him as she led the way. "Let's grab the girls and head upstairs."

Flynn obliged, picking up Beth and Alice. Mandy was content to latch on to Cindy. Upstairs, Cindy pointed out the room she'd chosen for Flynn. Although small, it was the least feminine one in the house. And directly next to it, she led them into a large bedroom, outfitted with three kid-size beds and an overflowing toy chest.

Squealing, the girls wriggled free and hurried over to the new bounty.

Overwhelmed, Flynn stared at her. "Cindy, you shouldn't have gone to so much trouble. This is too much."

She shrugged nonchalantly. "I do a lot of volunteer work and I bring home kids all the time so I had a lot of stuff."

"In threesomes?"

Cindy grinned. "Well, not exactly. But it wasn't that difficult to do a little rearranging."

He stared at the freshly painted pink walls, a captivating also newly painted mural, ruffled lace curtains and a newly upholstered window seat that matched the mural. "A *little* rearranging?"

"Okay. Guilty as charged. But I enjoyed doing it. And, really, cross my heart, I had the other kid paraphernalia."

Despite her protests, gratitude flooded him. Julia had lavished attention on her children, but they'd sorely missed a woman's touch since then.

"Look, Daddy!" Alice shouted, bringing him a bright pink-and-silver unicorn. The soft stuffed toy was toddler safe with no plastic eyes or nose for little ones to swallow.

He knelt down beside her. "That's nice, baby."

Happy with her treasure, Alice scooted away. Just as suddenly, Flynn felt exhausted. The past year had been an endless succession of trials and emotions. And now, without warning, Cindy had opened her life and home to them. It was as overwhelming as it was gratifying.

To his surprise, when he rose, he saw unexpected understanding in Cindy's expression. But she didn't comment on it. Instead, she smiled before turning to the triplets. "Okay, girls, we have tofu tacos for dinner. Who wants to eat?"

But the triplets were practically headfirst into the toy box.

"Probably should have told them about the tacos first," Cindy mused. "No matter." She glanced at Flynn. "Unless you're hungry?"

"I'd kill for some coffee."

She grinned. "You won't have to get that drastic. I could use some myself. Why don't we put up the safety gate at the top of the stairs and find our caffeine fix?"

"Won't get any argument from me," Flynn replied. But he made sure the safety gate was secure before he joined her in the farm-style kitchen.

He glanced around appreciatively. She had incorporated new appliances that resembled ones of yesteryear next to original freestanding cabinetry. She'd kept the integrity of the original structure, yet updated it enough to make it workable. He wondered what all the fronds of hanging dried herbs were for. Mixed among the bluish and sage green were also dried bouquets of roses and heather. It reminded him of a potently fragrant garden that had been preserved from past summers. "This is some kitchen."

"Thanks. It's one of my favorite rooms. I'm reworking them one at a time."

"You've got a pretty big house, Cindy. Planning on filling it up soon?"

For a moment she froze, her hands filled with a pitcher and carton of cream. Then she laughed, a nervous sound in the otherwise relaxed kitchen. "What makes you ask?"

"Just a comment on your home. I didn't mean to pry. Just thought maybe you were dating someone special."

Her fingers clenched the handle of the pitcher before she relaxed enough to pour the cream. "You have a vivid imagination."

"I thought maybe that was why you moved here."

Suddenly breathless, she made a production of looking for the sugar. "Excuse me?"

"I couldn't see any other reason for a young woman to move to the boonies. I thought it must be love."

"Love?" she asked, her voice sounding strangulated.

"I *am* prying. Sorry."

She fussed with the coffee cups, then added a plate of cookies to the tray before finally bringing it to the table. "No need to apologize."

"Still, it's a great house."

Cindy smiled. "Anything newer or smaller cost a fortune. Not many people want to fix up these old painted ladies. This one needed a lot of gutting and repair. Not to mention horrendous utility bills that are eating into my trust fund."

"You wouldn't trade it for a new one," he mused accurately, surprised to realize how

41

much she seemed to fit with the charming old house.

"Nope. It's drafty, always in need of fixing — and I love it."

He accepted the coffee she offered, studying the rose pattern of the fine bone china cup and saucer. "No generic mugs for you."

Her gaze followed his. "It's one of my weaknesses — collecting china. But I only have one complete set. I collect orphaned cups and saucers — I must have twenty of them, each a different pattern."

Flynn glanced at the other collectibles that lined her glass-fronted cabinets. "You like old things — antiques, I mean."

"They have history. I like to imagine the people who once owned them." She stared upward at the tall ceiling of the kitchen, then the original arched wooden-paned windows that brought the sunshine inside. "I couldn't imagine living in a house that's squeaky new, that hasn't had time to develop character."

"Like the one you convinced me to build," he commented wryly.

She flushed suddenly, not a gentle blush, but a violent wave of color, a shortcoming that seemed to be a side effect of being a redhead. "I'm sorry. I really didn't mean —"

But he dismissed her protest. "I know what you meant. And you're right. This house suits you. I'm just not sure yet what suits me." He'd known once, but everything about his life was uncertain now. Especially this move, the one that had him sitting next to her.

Compassion filled Cindy's eyes. "You'll know again, Flynn. It may not seem like it now, but you'll find your way."

"You sound remarkably certain."

"It's my faith," she explained gently. "It makes me sure there's a path for me. I might stumble now and then, but at the end of the day it's always there."

He nodded out of politeness, his own abandoned faith scarcely a bitter recollection.

Still, in comfortable silence they sipped the strong coffee and nibbled on buttery shortbread cookies.

Flynn cocked his ear, listening for the sounds of his daughters.

"I have a baby monitor," Cindy remembered suddenly. "I'll hook it up after dinner. In fact, it has enough units for all the bedrooms upstairs and one here in the kitchen."

Quizzical, Flynn studied her face. "Why do you have a baby monitor?"

"As I said, I bring home kids now and

then from my volunteer work. With a big old house like this, the monitor saves a lot of steps. One of the first little ones I brought home with me kept escaping from his crib. That's when I discovered baby monitors. Of course, with that little curtain climber, I could have used an alarm system."

An unexpected smile crossed Flynn's face. "That bad?"

"Unequivocally. And, of course, to make matters worse, he was an absolute charmer, so I could never stay mad more than a few seconds."

"That *would* be rough," Flynn remarked.

"Especially when it was time for him to go home. The house was deadly dull and I didn't get nearly enough exercise."

A thud from upstairs echoed through the floorboards. "I have a feeling you won't be lacking in exercise now." He stood. "I'll go check on them."

Cindy watched him leave, feeling her heartbeat settle to a near-normal rate. At this pace, she'd be a wreck in less than a day. Watching everything she said, trying not to read something into his words. . . . Briefly she closed her eyes, masking the questions. But not the big one. Had she made a terrible mistake in agreeing to let Flynn stay in her home? Would he somehow discern her hidden feelings? And could her heart stand this constant assault?

Again she heard a few thuds overheard, then the clatter of many small feet on the wooden stairs. Rounding up the troops, she realized.

In moments, the girls scampered into the kitchen and many of her apprehensions faded. How could she not give everything in her power to them? They were Julia's legacy, the only tangible link she had left. Little Mandy clutched Cindy's leg and the last of her reservations melted even more. Whatever it took, she would help these girls. No matter what it cost her own heart.

The following day, Flynn used a few rocks to anchor the blueprints on a portable camp table. Rudimentary but effective. The breeze was light, yet it ruffled the rolled paper just enough to keep it out of alignment.

Cindy glanced at the papers, then at the lot Flynn had purchased. "Are you happy with them? The architect drew up the plans awfully fast."

His gaze remained on the lot, but he didn't look especially pleased. Instead it was a contemplative expression. "Rand Miller's a friend. And he put together the complex for my insurance company."

"Does he design homes, too?"

"Usually bigger ones than I'm planning, but yes. He's doing this one as a favor to me."

"Has he seen the lot?" Cindy asked, her eyes on the triplets who seemed determined to pull up all the wild buttercups scattered across the field grass.

"We took a ride out here before he drew up the plans. Luckily, Linda showed me this lot first — so it didn't take any time to decide."

"The view's good," Cindy mused, appraising the gently knolled lot. "Are you planning to put the house at the top of the little hill?"

Flynn nodded. "That'll make the best use of the plans. I want a lot of windows — so many, it looks as though the walls are made of glass. Which works out well since I'm going to have a solar energy system."

Cindy pointed to the drawing of the roof. "This looks kind of unusual."

"Good eye," Flynn replied. "That's a cooling pool. With all the brush out here in the fields, there's a higher fire risk. The pool will keep the roof from catching a stray spark."

"Hmm."

Enjoying her polite but puzzled expression, Flynn laughed. "You don't sound convinced. It's not only for safety. We can swim in the pool, as well."

"Ah . . ." Politeness gave way to pleasure, softening her face in an unexpectedly attractive way.

Not that she wasn't already pretty. . . . Flynn felt his thoughts jerk in surprise. He'd always known what an attractive woman she was, but that had never mattered in the past. Not when Julia was alive. And because he and Cindy were all wrong for each other, it could never matter in the future.

"You'll be glad of that in the summer," Cindy was saying, her smile nearly as bright as her blazing hair.

"What's that?" he replied, distracted by the wash of unpleasant memories.

She drew her brows together as she glanced at him in quizzical surprise. "That you can swim in the pool."

"Oh . . . Yes."

But Cindy didn't seem to think his mental detour was significant. "The kids should love it."

His expression mellowed. "I want to build swing sets and a playhouse, too, make the house a place they want to be."

Cindy's smile was at once tender yet nostalgic. "You're a good father, Flynn."

But he couldn't easily accept the compliment. "I spent a lot of time away from them when they were babies. Julia was so competent. She and the girls were a perfect unit. It didn't seem as though she really needed me to be there." As soon as the words were out of his mouth, Flynn realized they were true. He'd never verbalized this vague feeling and it both surprised and embarrassed him that he'd made the confession to Cindy.

"Perhaps it just seemed that way," she suggested gently. "The way our parents died changed Julia forever. You know she blamed it on their incurable zest for adventure." Cindy paused, her expression reflective. "And I always felt that was why she became so efficient and capable. So much so that she no doubt thought taking charge of the girls was good for both of you. And she probably didn't realize she was radiating such a self-sufficient image."

"Maybe," Flynn acknowledged, not completely buying the explanation. Cindy was right about their parents. Julia had confided early on that's why she wanted stability and security, but it didn't explain shutting him out. "I should have seen past that, made sure I was involved in raising my own children."

Cindy moved a bit closer. "The important thing is that you're here for the girls now. As difficult as this sounds, they probably don't remember any of that earlier time."

He nodded glumly, suspecting it wouldn't be long before they lost all memory of their mother.

"Oh, Flynn! You don't think they'll forget their mother, do you?" Cindy exclaimed, obviously only that very moment realizing they could forget Julia.

But he couldn't find any glib reassurances to offer. "I've worried about it. Even now, they speak of her less and less often."

Dismayed, Cindy stared at him, tears misting her vivid green eyes, as she brought one hand to her mouth.

Flynn moved closer, his fingers closing around her arm. "Between us they'll remember." It was as much a promise as a resolution. A promise born of one he'd made long ago.

"She loved them so much," Cindy murmured. "They have to know that."

"They'll see it in you," Flynn told her, the response surprising both of them.

Cindy's chin lifted, her eyes meeting his. "They will?"

"They've held an attachment to you

that's remarkable, considering how young they are, how seldom you used to see them. I can't help but think it's your connection to their mother."

Slowly, almost painfully, Cindy nodded. "There was a time when Julia and I were so close, we used to imagine we were twins."

Flynn frowned, the words giving him weighty pause. "You never seemed much alike to me."

A smile rose from the pain on her face. "Probably not to anyone else. We don't look anything alike — I'm the only renegade redhead besides my grandmother. And I'm as boisterous as Julia was refined, but it was something deeper. A connection in our souls. And that only strengthened after our parents died."

"But you didn't visit all that often. And you moved away from Houston," he pointed out, wondering yet again about his elusive sister-in-law, remembering how he'd shut out any thoughts of her once Julia was his.

Cindy turned, her gaze fastening on the gently winding road that was nearly obscured by the great tracts of irrepressible wild grass. Her open expression didn't slam shut; rather it sidled away so subtly, he wondered if he imagined the change.

"People grow up and away," she finally answered. "Distance need not be more than a physical impediment. I don't think it was for us."

"She missed you," Flynn admitted. "Especially since you were the last of your family."

Pain vaulted past subtlety, ravishing her face. "I had no idea."

"Don't take the words to heart. But you should know how she felt, how she always valued your relationship." He couldn't admit that Cindy's absence from their lives had been a relief to him. Flynn hadn't needed or wanted reminders of what she represented, of what he had tried to escape every day since childhood.

Despite his reassurance, only a sparse bit of comfort mixed with the trepidation painting her face. "I should have visited more. I shouldn't have let . . ."

"What?" he asked, when her words trailed away.

She brushed a tear from the corner of her eye, then shook her head. "Nothing."

"Did you have an argument?" Flynn asked, wondering how he could have not known that.

"No." For a moment her face brightened. "Julia wouldn't have allowed it. Besides, she was my other half. Surely you've noticed that we were complete opposites?"

The fact that Cindy was her sister's opposite in every way was still Cindy's biggest downfall in his opinion, the reason he'd chosen Julia over her, yet he nodded.

"We seemed to complete what the other lacked. And I feel like my other half's gone forever." Suddenly she looked horrified. "I don't know what's wrong with me. I keep putting both feet in my mouth and tromping around like they're clad in combat boots. I'm so sorry. You truly have lost your other half."

"No need to apologize. We both lost her." His gaze moved to include the girls, who were tossing wildflowers skyward, then giggling madly as the blossoms fell down upon them. "We all did."

"Children are so resilient," Cindy mused. "It's one of the ways the Lord protects them."

Flynn lifted his eyebrows but he didn't respond, thinking it wasn't worth arguing over. His own faith was long gone, and he still believed it wasn't something Cindy would be spouting for long. "Hmm."

But Cindy didn't argue in defense. Instead, the expression in her eyes was so knowing and certain it defused any debate.

At once, Flynn felt old defenses lock into place.

As his thoughts rumbled, he spotted the girls as they started running toward the road. Even though only a handful of cars had passed in the last hour, Flynn and Cindy both bolted after them. It didn't take long to corral the children.

"All right, girls, you know better than to run toward the road," Flynn began in a stern tone.

But the girls laughed as they jumped up and down, cutting off his reprimand.

Since where they stood was still plenty of distance from the street, Flynn tried not to overreact.

"Cows!" Alice hollered, pointing across the road.

Glancing up, Flynn saw a mild-mannered herd of dairy cattle munching on the grass. "So that was the attraction," he muttered.

"You have to be wary of small-town dangers," Cindy agreed in a serious tone. But the twinkle in her eyes gave her away.

"They do look pretty ferocious," Flynn replied, seeing the cattle's only movement was the swishing of hairy tails and the methodical chewing of cud.

A tiny giggle escaped even though Cindy was clearly trying to keep it under control.

"We have some wild ice-cream socials here in town, too. Gotta be on your guard all the time."

Flynn glanced down the empty road. "I can see that. There might even be a horse or two in the next pasture over."

"Horsie!" Beth and Mandy repeated in delight.

"Cow!" Alice insisted.

"Just wait until a new movie comes to town." Cindy couldn't repress her grin. "The excitement's enough to do you in."

"I think for now the horses and cows will keep us entertained."

Cindy's expression was knowing and skeptical. "We'll talk in six months when the biggest action in town is the fall carnival."

"I haven't been to a carnival since I was a kid." The thought was unexpectedly warming. But Flynn knew what Cindy was driving at. Clearly she thought he would grow tired of small-town life, that Rosewood would lose its appeal. But everything else that had once held appeal for him was now gone. Yet instinctively he felt that the tiny town was right for him. Was it possible he'd been given another chance? Another place to call home?

Chapter Three

†

"I'm on to you guys," Cindy told the girls with mock seriousness as she wiped one face, only to see another triplet smear granola cereal across her cheek.

They only giggled more.

Each of the girls was secured in a booster seat, bowls and spoons in the same vicinity, as they sat around the breakfast table with Cindy.

"Here you are," Flynn greeted them. Awakening only moments earlier, he'd been startled to find all three girls gone from their beds. Passing Cindy's room, which was next to the girls', he could see it was empty, as well.

Cindy and his daughters glanced up at him in unison. The girls garbled out greetings mixed with cereal and juice, slurry versions of "Daddy."

"Morning," Cindy greeted him.

Flynn was unable to shake the frown from his face. "You didn't have to do this."

She shrugged easily. "No big deal. I was up, they got up. So we're eating."

"But they're a lot of trouble to feed and —"

"Not really. Besides, it's more fun than eating by myself with only the newspaper for company."

"Oh." Deflated, he wasn't certain what to say. For the past year, despite a house-keeper, nannies and sitters, much of his daughters' care had fallen on him. It was disconcerting to see how easily Cindy took over the chore. "They weren't up this early the last few days."

"Takes a while to get settled into a new place. And it's possible I woke them when I got up."

"I didn't hear anything."

"You're two rooms over. Besides, like I said, it's no big deal. Actually, it's kind of fun." Mandy decorated her golden, honey-blond hair that moment with a glob of cereal. Cindy laughed aloud as she reached for a damp towel. "For the most part, anyway."

"I'm up. I can take over."

"Why don't you grab some coffee?" Cindy smoothed the towel gently over Mandy's hair, removing most of the cereal. "No sense jumping in till you're awake." She stood just then, moving over to the re-frigerator, drawing out a container of or-ganic apple juice.

His mouth opened as he intended to tell her to back off, that these were *his* children, that *he* would feed them breakfast. She spun around, however, at that moment her face pulling into a tentative look of speculation. "You know, I may have to take you up on that offer. I got so caught up in the girls I forgot today is Tuesday, my Rainbow class day."

Pottery, he guessed, or some similar sort of thing. She'd always been involved in one crazy project after another. Julia had reported on her sister's escapades often enough. But that had only reinforced his opinion. Cindy was fun, reckless and totally without responsibility. He'd finally stopped listening to Julia's tales, having learned enough about Cindy. He had grown up in a home where fun had been valued over stability and it had ruined all their lives. It was the reason he'd always remained detached from Cindy. Now she was offering him back the responsibility for the girls so she could run off to some mindless class. "Fine."

She smiled. "I have a few minutes, though, if you'd like that coffee."

His voice sounded stiff even to his own ears. "It's not necessary. I *have* managed to feed them and drink my coffee for the past year."

Her brows drew together. "Of course, but —"

The phone rang, cutting off her reply.

Flynn could only hear one end of the conversation, but he didn't need to listen long to learn that it sounded as though she planned to meet half a dozen friends for the day's outing.

"Fine, I'll pick up Lisa and Heather on the way, too," Cindy continued on the phone. She glanced at her watch. "But I'd better run." She turned back to Flynn after clicking off the phone. "You sure you're okay on your own? I could make some arrangements if —"

"No. I told you I didn't want our staying here to interfere with your life."

"It's not. It's just that today —"

"Go," he replied shortly, sliding into the chair nestled between the girls.

Looking as though she wanted to continue what she was saying, instead Cindy nodded. "I'll see you later, then."

That was more like it, he thought to himself after she left the kitchen. He hadn't asked for or wanted Cindy's help. Turning back to the girls, he saw that they weren't happy with her disappearance, though.

"Cinny," they wailed in unison.

"Daddy's here." He comforted them.

"Cinny!" they continued demanding.

"Cereal?" he questioned, pushing a measure of enthusiasm into his voice, staring down at the unfamiliar granola, thinking it didn't look very appetizing.

But when he glanced up, three minor storms had descended over their faces.

"It wasn't my idea for her to leave," he attempted.

Beth, always the loudest of the triplets, banged her spoon on the edge of the table. "Cinny!"

"Okay, time to settle down and eat your breakfast."

Although they weren't happy with the request, they eventually complied. Three sticky faces later, he was near the end of his patience. It was going to take forever to get the girls cleaned up, not to mention the damage they'd done to Cindy's formerly spotless kitchen floor. It wasn't how he'd anticipated the day, but there was no getting around the fact. He was going to be scraping up granola for at least part of the morning.

Cindy was tired. Her usually endless supply of energy was running low. It had started draining that morning when Flynn pulled his stiff, get-out-of-my-face act. She'd tried to repump, knowing the

Rainbow children needed all she had to give. But his mood had intruded on hers the entire day — even though today had also been filled with rewards.

None of them was the large variety that impressed most people. Rather the small ones, like when Heather offered to share a toy. Not remarkable for most children. But then Heather wasn't the average child. She'd lost her parents and younger brother in a car accident. Now, living with an aunt and uncle who didn't really want her, she'd become hostile, desocialized. A few months earlier Cindy had convinced the child's guardians to allow Heather to attend the Rainbow class.

The class had begun three years earlier with one lonesome little girl, Lana, the child of a single father who was desperate to round out his daughter's life with the happiness she'd lost along with her mother. Cindy, full of love she'd yet to give anyone, lavished it on Lana, finally coaxing smiles, then laughter from her sad little face. Then another emotionally scarred child had come along. And another.

Katherine had encouraged Cindy when she'd suggested forming a group. And the Rainbow class was born. Children continued to join, all with a variety of needs, no two the same. Yet they came together in the Rainbow class, a healing, nurturing place.

Normally days spent with her "Rainbow" kids were ones of great satisfaction. But the nagging feelings she'd carried with her from the house had stolen some of that pleasure.

As she pulled into her driveway, Cindy couldn't halt a jolt of apprehension. It wasn't a simple emotion, but one tied in to her feelings for Flynn, his obvious dissatisfaction and the grand mess she'd made by inviting him to stay in her house.

For the first time since purchasing the winsome Victorian, she was reluctant to enter. Her throat caught — this, her place of refuge, was no longer a sanctuary. Forcing the dregs of her energy to respond, she pushed open the front door.

And entered chaos.

The triplets, who appeared to have dragged every toy in the house to the front hall and parlor, were running through both rooms as though flung like buckshot.

Paralyzed for a moment, she watched in stupefied fascination as Flynn entered the hall and tried to harness the girls.

He glanced up just then, all his earlier stiff resentment gone, replaced by a sheepish embarrassment. "It's really not as bad as it looks."

She placed her purse on the hall table. "That's a relief."

"Nothing's broken — I put all the fragile stuff up high." Cindy glanced at her assortment of antique scarves and shawls that normally hung from a brass rack near the door. Apparently the triplets had tugged them free. Now they were strung haphazardly over and across the rich marquetry floors. Sunlight from the second-story rotunda usually shone on the intricate pattern of oak, bird's-eye maple and rare East Texas long leaf pine. Now, however, it was hardly visible under the mess.

"Things got a little out of control," Flynn admitted.

"So I see."

Flynn followed her gaze, releasing a low groan. "I didn't realize they'd gotten into your scarves, as well. To be honest, I thought once I'd put the breakables out of reach, they'd be safe while I mopped the kitchen floor."

Amazed, she stared at him. "Why did you feel you had to mop the floor? I just did it —"

"Breakfast," he explained, the one word conveying paragraphs.

"Oh."

He met her gaze. "I know I said I didn't need any help, rather emphatically if I remember correctly. Truth is, back home we had a housekeeper. While she wasn't their nanny, she kept all the messes and spills cleaned up. I never realized how difficult it would be to watch the girls *and* clean up their fallout."

She felt a chuckle unexpectedly germinating and tried to suppress it. "Sometimes things aren't as easy as they appear."

He glanced around the nearly destroyed area. "I'd say that was an understatement. Unless you have a strong objection, I'd like to find a housekeeper as soon as possible."

Cindy allowed a fraction of her smile to escape. "I don't think that's really necessary."

"You want to live like this?"

"That's not necessary, either." She kept her tone mild, guessing the end of his rope was nearly frayed. "I often have four or five children here at one time. But it does take a little organization, some planning."

He stared at her in disbelief.

"I *do* have a grasp on those concepts," she told him wryly.

"Still —"

She held up one hand. "I'm really not accustomed to depending on others, especially in my own home. To be honest, it would seem like an intrusion. How about if we try it my way for, say, a week? If it doesn't work, we'll look into finding a housekeeper."

"A *week?*"

She chuckled. "You sound about the girls' age. It's a week, not a year."

"Maybe so. But the week I'm anticipating will seem like a year."

Cindy bent down, retrieving a hand-beaded silk shawl that was the prize of her collection. "Look at it this way. Your stuff's in storage so I've got the most to lose."

"Point taken. I just hope you don't regret your offer."

Regret. It was her constant companion, a reminder she couldn't shake with hurricane force winds. But having become an expert at disguising her feelings, she only smiled, edging toward the kitchen. "I'd better check things out, start on dinner."

"The floor's clean," he responded.

She glanced at the wreckage in the parlor and hall and nodded. "Well, that's one positive."

"Don't worry, Cindy. I'll put things back to rights."

She disappeared into the kitchen. It wasn't possible, she knew. Even if the house was fashioned into *Architectural Digest* perfection, things could never be made right.

Not while he held her heart in his hands, and didn't even realize he controlled its very rhythm.

Dinner was spectacularly uneventful. Only a few spoonfuls of mashed peas landed on the floor, soon wiped clean. Flynn wasn't certain just how Cindy had accomplished it, but control prevailed throughout the meal. But it wasn't a disciplinary nightmare. To the contrary, the girls were happy, easy to handle.

Perhaps it was a woman thing, he mused. Julia had always had just the right touch with the girls, as well. But that wasn't something he expected Cindy to share with her sister.

Bathtime was also competently and quickly accomplished. Soon, the girls were snuggled in their sleepers, tucked into their matching beds.

More than a bit amazed, Flynn studied Cindy as they reached the bottom of the stairwell. He wondered if she was part magician, making the care of the triplets seem effortless.

Having reassembled much of the parlor, he began gathering some of the scarves still strewn across the floor.

Cindy stooped down, as well, carefully

picking up each ancient slip of fabric.

"These are really . . . different," Flynn finally decided aloud.

"That doesn't exactly sound like a compliment."

He held up one sheer red scarf, threaded with gold, edged with long strands of dark fringe. "They suit you."

Her smile was wry. "Again, I'm not sure that's a compliment."

Flynn paused, the scarf awkwardly filling his hands. "Look, I know we don't see many things the same way." He held up the exotic red silk. "But I don't have any frame of reference for stuff like this."

"Granted," she replied, a touch of a sigh flavoring the solitary word. "Julia was always practical, unlike me. Cotton versus silk, that was us."

He studied the weariness she couldn't quite disguise. "We haven't gotten off to the best start, have we?"

She shrugged. "It's a big adjustment. You're used to running things your way."

"And you're used to being on your own."

Cindy lifted her face, new shadows deepening her obvious fatigue. "Yes. That I am."

Flynn sighed. "I knew this was a bad idea. We're messing up your life, your home."

"I'm not a neat freak," she replied after the barest pause. Then her eyes shifted away. "We knew going in this wasn't an ideal situation, but if it helps the girls, I can manage. How about you?"

He fingered the soft, exotic scarf. "I'll do whatever it takes to make the girls happy."

"Then there's no more to say," she responded.

Flynn wanted to search her eyes, to see how Cindy really felt, but she stood, turning to the brass rack. He owed her an apology, but it was difficult to spit out. He'd spent the better part of his adult life making certain he had nothing else to be sorry for. And he doubted even his unsettling sister-in-law could change that.

Cindy chose to be especially quiet the following morning as she worked in the downstairs conservatory. Not wanting a repeat of Flynn's displeasure, she'd tiptoed around her bedroom as she'd dressed, then slipped silently down the stairs, knowing how to avoid the creaks in the ancient steps.

Her night had been restless, filled with dreams caused by thoughts she couldn't chase away. So she'd risen early to escape them, needing to lose herself in activity.

Picking up a box filled with old photos, she started to put it aside. Then she glanced at the picture on top. Settling the box on top of the table, she withdrew the photo. It had been taken years ago. Her parents, Julia and herself. They were on vacation at Disneyland. Julia and their mother both looked pretty, smiling gracefully. But Cindy and her father were wearing goofy hats and glasses, wide, silly grins covering their faces. She eased a thumb over the slick surface, remembering the good times, the pain of loss that had faded, but never disappeared.

Flynn coughed from the doorway.

Startled, Cindy dropped the photograph.

He entered, reaching down to pick it up before she could. "Nice picture."

She nodded, not willing to delve into her unreconciled loss. "Kind of early in the morning for reminiscing, isn't it?"

"I wasn't actually. Just saw that picture and it brought back a lot of memories."

He looked at it again. "You and Julia were on different wavelengths."

Cindy swallowed the pain of that comment. "She was always more like Mother, refined, graceful, elegant."

"And you were like your father?"

"I guess so. He was the adventurer — the one who wildcatted after the days of oil wildcatting were past. He liked to pursue the impossible."

Flynn's gaze shifted between Cindy and the picture. "I'm not like my mother, either."

Never having heard much about his family, she wondered about them. "What was she like?"

His face closed. Tossing down the picture, he shrugged. "Just a mother." Then he glanced at the newly cleared desk. "What are you doing in here?"

"Making a temporary office for you."

His eyes swept over the newly arranged room. "You didn't have to do this —"

"You're beginning to sound like a broken record," she interrupted. "You need a place to work in until you get the office space you want."

"I'm hoping to get that set up soon."

"Fine. I'll need the room back after a while anyway. It's one I use sometimes for one of my volunteer functions. And in the future it may be the permanent spot for the class."

He frowned. "Then why go to so much trouble?"

This time she didn't shift her gaze, instead meeting his. "It's who I am."

He studied her, clearly baffled.

But then that was the point. She'd always baffled and alienated him. And moving to Rosewood wasn't going to change his impression. Only reinforce it.

Chapter Four

†

Two days later, Flynn pushed aside the sage-green sheers that covered the tall conservatory windows. Tapestry drapes that puddled beyond the woodwork onto the floor were tied back with thick, silky tassels. It seemed Cindy left no detail unattended. Two pairs of aged leather wing chairs were grouped beside a small fireplace. And a Georgian library table served as a desk, covered by neat stacks of his work papers.

Like the rest of the house, this room was cozy. He was no decorator, but the furnishings she chose reminded him of older homes he'd visited in England and France. Even the landscapes and botanical prints looked as though they could be European in origin.

It was restful, snug and casual, yet he itched with discomfort. He glanced down at the candy bowl filled with sunflower and pumpkin seeds. The house and the temporary office suited him no better than the birdseed she called food.

From the window he could see the swish of a weeping willow in the gentle breeze.

And across the street, an elderly gentleman handled his roses with the care usually reserved for rare orchids.

A knock, so quiet it barely penetrated the thick mahogany door, reached him. He turned. "Come in."

Cindy, looking somewhat like a wary red-headed comet, poked her head in. "Do you need anything?"

Flynn shook his head. "I don't know what it would be."

"Enough paper? A snack? Maybe some coffee?"

Although he appreciated her concern, he'd never been comfortable accepting help. "Cindy, I'm not accustomed to having someone make all my decisions for me."

She blanched for a moment. "I didn't realize an offer of coffee constituted interfering."

Flynn drew one hand back across his hair. "That's not what I'm talking about."

Her green eyes still looked stormy. "Then what?"

He gestured around the room, overwhelmed and embarrassed by her generosity. "This. Everything. I didn't ask for an office, but you produced one anyway. Even after I told you I didn't want it."

Cindy's fingers curled around the edge of

the door. "You don't have to use it," she replied evenly. "After all, you've rented another office. If you don't mind moving in there while they're renovating, I certainly don't."

The pull and tug vibrated between them. Suddenly half a dozen small footsteps thudded across the floor. "Cinny! Daddy!"

As the triplets approached, Cindy turned, ending the immediate need for resolution. She knelt as the girls reached her. "Why don't we go swing in the backyard? Let Daddy work."

"You've been taking care of the girls all day. Why don't I take them outside?"

"I want Cinny!" Beth retorted.

Cindy glanced between Flynn and his daughters. "If your daddy helps you swing, I could set the table in the backyard and we could have supper there."

"Supper?" Mandy asked.

"Veggie burgers," Cindy replied. "They're yummy."

Flynn didn't agree, but also didn't want to snap her olive branch in half.

"Yummy," Alice repeated.

He glanced at his daughters, more content in the last week than the last year. For that he could eat veggie burgers and granola. He could also somehow find a compromise with Cindy.

"And I'm about done with work for today," he added, finding a second note of accord.

"Wanna make yummies," Alice was requesting.

Cindy ran gentle fingers through her blond curls. "I can always use a good helper."

"Good helper me," Alice agreed.

"So you are."

"Wanna swing with Daddy," Beth stated more assertively.

"Me, too," Mandy spoke up.

Flynn walked toward them, stretching his hands out toward the girls.

Beth and Mandy readily placed their small hands within his. Seeing the unsettled look that remained on Cindy's face, Flynn relented. "Veggie burgers, huh? I don't suppose we could have French fries with those?"

Unexpectedly her lips twitched. "To cancel out the healthy effect of the meal's veggie portion?"

"Something like that," he agreed. "I'm more a meat-and-potatoes kind of guy."

Her smile widened. "Is that why you pick all the sprouts out of the salad?"

He winced. "I thought I was a touch more subtle."

"Not especially."

Surprise melted away the last of his reserve. "No kind demur?"

"No. That would have been someone else. Not me."

Julia, he knew. Cindy wouldn't say it in front of the girls, but it was true. Julia had always smoothed over any potential bump that could have put a ripple in any conversation. It had been the tone of their entire relationship.

Flynn walked outside with his daughters, losing himself for the moment beneath the cover of towering oaks and ivy-covered lattice work. The yard smelled of honeysuckle vines that poked fragrant blooms through the cracks of the weathered fence. The swing set that sat on the longish grass was old, not new and shiny. But it was so sturdy, it could hold eight children; now it only needed to support his two small daughters.

Glancing back toward the house, Flynn wondered what it was about his sister-in-law that commanded such affection from his children. Alice had always clung the closest to him, never wanting to be separated. Beth might toddle off on her own, Mandy sometimes only a few feet behind. But not Alice. She was Daddy's girl.

Only, now she seemed to be Cindy's girl.

Inside, Cindy allowed Alice to pat and roll the burgers into shape. They were beginning to resemble small boulders.

"A Flintstones supper, Alice? Good job." After washing the child's hands, Cindy led her to the ancient French doors that opened to the backyard. "Why don't you go swing for a while with Beth and Mandy?"

Happy to be with both Cindy and her father, Alice scampered contentedly away. Watching her, Cindy couldn't help but wonder if all memories of Julia were fading from their young minds. For a moment she felt a stab of longing for her deceased sister, one more poignant than she'd felt since her untimely death. Even now, Cindy railed against the unfairness.

Colon cancer had struck silently, without warning. And Julia, in typical fashion, had persisted in acting as though nothing could go wrong with her perfect life, her perfect family. Ignoring the final, irreversible symptoms, she had died within six weeks of the diagnosis.

Julia's little family was adrift. In Cindy's backyard. Peering out the large windows, she saw how gentle Flynn was with his daughters. It was a side he showed only with them. Cindy couldn't even remember seeing him treat Julia with the same tenderness. His manner toward Julia had always been filled with deep respect and devotion, but not tenderness. It was as though he'd placed Julia on a pedestal — one her sister had relished. Suddenly she wondered why.

The girls' giggles floated through the open French doors. The low murmur of Flynn's voice accompanied the happy sound. Even though she couldn't understand the walls he constructed or the reasons for them, Cindy could see the joy he brought out in the girls. Although reluctant to cease her uncensored view, she gathered the charcoal lighter and matches.

Once outside, Flynn spotted her as she approached the grill. "I'll start the fire," he offered.

"Great. My least favorite part of eating outside." She handed him the supplies, checking quickly to see that the girls were still safe.

Within a few minutes Flynn had a good fire going. Cindy rounded up condiments and place settings. However, when she brought out the plate containing the misshapen burgers, he raised his brows.

"Pretend we're in Bedrock," she told him breezily.

"I'm still getting fries, right?"

She nodded.

"Fine. We can be in Oz then for all I care."

It was so out of character for Flynn that she paused. Musing, she returned to the kitchen to prepare his French fries.

By the time she brought them to the table, Flynn had finished grilling the burgers. The girls ran from the swings, their short legs pumping with the effort.

Once they were seated, and their burgers assembled, Flynn and Cindy concentrated on their own plates.

He stared at his burger with a noticeable lack of enthusiasm. "Do you have something against regular food?"

"*Regular* food?" she repeated. "As in cholesterol-clogging, energy-draining junk food?"

He took a hefty portion of French fries. "Absolutely." Tasting one, his expression changed. "Are these made some . . . uh . . . special way?"

"They're made from potatoes and they're fried," she replied enigmatically.

"In what?"

"Olive and canola oil," she admitted.

He sighed. "Does everything you cook have to be so . . . healthy?"

She took a moment's pity on him. "We do have a fast-food joint in town. You can always get a fix there."

He picked up another fry, his words hesitant. "You've been doing all the cooking and I don't sound very grateful."

Cindy felt the saddening, one that came from a place she could never quite conquer. "It's not what you're used to." Smiling to hide the pain, she glanced down at the simple dinner. "None of it. Me, this house, the food you think suits birds and squirrels better than people. You probably feel as though you've landed on another planet."

He glanced at the girls, but they were more interested in spearing pickles than the adult conversation. "It is different," he finally admitted. "But I needed a change. And the girls wanted Aunt Cinny."

Caution slid past logic. "They'd have forgotten me in time."

He glanced up, catching her eyes.

"Yes," she replied to the unspoken question there. "Like they're forgetting much of the past year."

In the quiet, the chirp of early-evening crickets mingled with the girls' random giggles and murmurs.

"Are you already tired of us?" he questioned in a low tone that didn't carry down the table.

She could say so much, so very much. Her gaze flew to the girls, cheerfully smearing Cindy's homemade mayonnaise on the table. Correction, she couldn't say anything at all. "No. It's great having the girls here." She paused. "And you, of course. The house is full of noise and smiles and laughter. I wouldn't trade that for anything." She wouldn't, Cindy realized, despite the heartache. It wasn't simply an empty assurance for Flynn.

"Veggie burgers are probably good for us," he offered finally.

Cindy's laugh spilled between them. "Then you'll love the carob-chip cookies."

"I don't suppose you have any genuine chocolate in the house."

She tried to resist the pull of his eyes. "Well, I'm not a fanatic!"

"So you can be tempted?"

Oh, so tempted. She scrambled for a reasonable reply. "I eat the way I do because I like it, not to prove a point."

"Do you ever eat out?"

"Of course. I'm willing to try most anything."

His expression was reflective.

When he didn't reply, she prodded him. "What?"

He shook his head. "Nothing really. Just that Julia never wanted to try anything new."

Of course not. Steady, dependable Julia never made Flynn grimace in displeased surprise. "That must have been a comfort."

"Yes," he agreed.

His reply took away her words, her desire to keep the conversation flowing. She was so everything Julia wasn't. So everything Flynn despised.

The following day Flynn examined the progress on the office space he had rented. The renovations weren't coming along as quickly as he'd hoped. Although they were only weeks from completion, he wished it were mere days. He needed to get his office out of Cindy's house.

Never having had to wrestle with a woman over the issue of control, he found himself uncertain how to deal with Cindy.

Julia had never questioned his opinions, in fact preferring to let him assume all the responsibility and worry of their decisions. It had become their custom for him to decide and for her to comply. It irritated him that Cindy had him wondering if that had always been for the best.

A knock sounded on the outer door. "Hello, anyone here?" a man called out.

"In here," Flynn responded, rounding the corner.

A tall, dark-haired man approached, extending his hand. "I'm Michael Carlson."

"Flynn Mallory," he responded automatically.

"Katherine's Carlson's husband," the man continued.

Flynn searched his memory.

But Michael began to grin. "I see that my wife and her friend didn't tell you about this visit."

Flynn shook his head.

"Katherine and Cindy are friends."

"Oh, the pastor," Flynn remembered.

Michael's grin spread. "Yeah, that's what I thought at first, too."

"Sorry, I —"

"It's okay. Most people aren't used to women ministers. Actually, Cindy asked me if I could stop by, take a look at your renovations. She said your contractor's behind on the job."

"Oh." Flynn issued the solitary word.

"I see she didn't tell you. Listen, if you'd rather call someone else, fine by me."

"I need to get this place operational as soon as possible. But you've probably got a lot of important jobs to be overseeing rather than looking at this dinky office."

Michael shook his head. "I work on all kinds of jobs. I do a lot of remodeling as well as building stores, offices, the new headquarters for Adair Petroleum. And like I said, Cindy asked."

"And that's all it took?"

"Yeah, pretty much."

Flynn couldn't hide his surprise. "Guess things work differently in a small town than a place like Houston."

"I imagine so. All I've known are small towns. I didn't grow up in Rosewood, but a place pretty close in size." Michael looked around at the partially demolished space. "So, what's this going to be?"

Flynn smiled. "Software Development."

Michael nodded. "And you can run that kind of business from anywhere. Rosewood's as perfect as Silicon Valley."

Flynn studied the other man with new respect. "My thoughts exactly."

"You've picked a good town, lots of good people here."

"That's what Cindy's been telling me."

Michael studied him. "But you're not sure yet. That's okay. I don't judge an orange by its peel, either. Get to know us first."

Flynn wasn't accustomed to this much directness, but it struck a chord. "Good advice."

Michael's gaze roamed around the building. "Now, let's see if you like the rest of it."

Hours later, Flynn headed back to Cindy's house. Michael Carlson had carefully examined the office structure. Then he'd offered to have a word with the contractor Flynn had hired. But Flynn wasn't comfortable accepting help from strangers. Or friends for that matter.

Even though he hadn't appreciated Cindy's interference, Flynn liked Michael. Instinctively Flynn believed he was honest, capable.

Still, that brought him round to why Cindy had asked Michael to stop by. Why she felt a need for control, one he hated to admit equalled his own.

Entering the house, he didn't hear anyone; in fact it seemed deadly still. The panic that had struck him once as a child and never fully disappeared now crawled into his throat.

His walk a near run, he traveled through

84

the front rooms, finally jogging into the kitchen. He was ready to turn back and tear up the stairs, when he heard the hum of voices from the backyard. The French doors were closed. Only one kitchen window was slightly ajar, dimming the sounds.

Pulling open the doors, he searched for and saw his daughters. Relieved, he watched for a moment as they played with three children he hadn't seen before.

And in the background Cindy's distinctive, upbeat voice blended with that of another woman's. Flynn took a few steps forward.

It was bright in the yard, the warming spring sunshine pushing past overhanging branches, muted only by the slats of the faded white lattice arbors. And Cindy sat in the sunshine and shadow.

There was something different about her, he realized, walking farther into the yard. Fully animated, unreserved, she was as brilliant as the deep fuchsia azaleas blooming around her.

Glancing up, she spotted him, and some of her vivacity faded. Still, she smiled in welcome.

"Hello, ladies," he greeted them.

Her friend tossed back long dark hair and

extended her hand. "I'm Katherine Carlson. I've heard so much about you and your daughters. It's a real pleasure to meet you."

He hesitated for a moment, amazed that this attractive woman was the "female preacher."

She noticed and her grin widened. "Yep. It's true. I'm the woman minister."

He collected his manners, shaking her proffered hand. "No wonder your husband looks like such a happy man."

Confident, unflappable Katherine blushed.

Cindy, to his surprise, winked at him with an equally wide grin. "Then I guess that means Michael found you this morning."

Katherine recovered a trace of her composure. "I hope he was able to help. Michael subcontracts out a lot of the smaller jobs. If your contractor's one of those, he would probably listen to Michael."

Flynn met Cindy's eyes. "I do want to get things going quickly. I'm not comfortable working from Cindy's house."

Katherine shrugged. "Beats me why anyone would rather work in an office building than this charming place, but I'm sure Michael could help if you ask him."

"That's great," Cindy concurred, not relinquishing Flynn's gaze. "I'll be needing the conservatory for one of my groups soon anyway."

Katherine glanced between them, but didn't comment on the visible tension. "Looks like the kids are getting along well."

Belatedly Flynn and Cindy pulled their gazes from each other.

"So it does," Flynn agreed, wishing Cindy wouldn't look at him that way. There was no reason to feel guilty about telling the truth. Then he really looked at the kids. "How old are your children?"

Katherine's face softened. "David's the oldest. He's eight. Annie's six. And baby Danny's fourteen months."

Flynn watched them for a few more minutes. "The older ones are good with your youngest and my girls, as well."

"They've always treated Danny as though they found him under the tree on Christmas morning," Katherine replied with a winsome laugh. "But then, since he was a gift from God, that's not so bad."

Flynn swallowed the comment that sprang to mind. He didn't have to agree with people to remain polite. "Still, you should be proud of them. Older children aren't always so gentle with toddlers."

Surprisingly Katherine's eyes brightened

with an unexpected sheen of tears. "I'm so proud of them I could burst. Annie, David, Danny and their father are the best things that ever happened to me."

Cindy's gaze suddenly held red-hot warning. So he chose his words carefully. "My girls mean the world to me, too."

Katherine recovered her composure. "I know. Cindy's told me about your late wife, and all the sacrifices you made to move to Rosewood."

Startled, Flynn stared at Cindy.

However, her expression didn't lighten. In fact, if he could identify the emotion lurking there, it would be suspicion. And for the life of him, he didn't know what caused that.

"Mommy!" Annie hollered, running up to them, all dark hair and huge blue eyes. Seeing Flynn, she turned suddenly shy.

"Hi," he said first. "I'm Flynn. You must be Annie."

She bobbed her head up and down. "Uh-huh. Can the girls swing with me?"

Katherine stood. "How about if I super-vise?" she asked Flynn.

He agreed and in moments he was alone with Cindy. "Is something wrong?"

She studied him. How could she tell him she still had doubts about his uncharacter-

88

istic move to Rosewood? She felt a desperate need to safeguard the life she'd built, afraid that her heart would outweigh her caution. Knowing none of it could be said, instead she shook her head. "No. I just didn't expect you home so soon. I thought you wanted to work in your new office space."

"About that . . . Why did you ask Michael Carlson to come by, without telling me?"

Exasperated, she all but snorted. "Are we back to that again? Are you a total control freak?"

"Not any more than you apparently."

She counted inwardly to ten. "I *know* I'm not like Julia. I'm sure she deferred to your every comment and dictate. But I don't operate that way. I *do* have opinions. And while I don't always insist they're right, I intend to express them." Cindy paused. "Well, unless they hurt someone's feelings, of course. But I'm not retiring and complacent. I have ideas. I make my own decisions." She met his gaze, feeling her chest tighten. "And I'm not going to try to be someone I'm not."

"I don't recall asking you to," he replied mildly. "But I would appreciate a heads-up when you send someone like Michael over."

She frowned. "Didn't you like him?"

"That's not the point."

"*Everybody* likes Michael," she responded in instant defense, never forgetting how happy he had made her once-lonely best friend.

"Are you being deliberately obtuse?" Flynn asked. "I'm only asking that you not blindside me."

"Then you did like Michael?" she asked hopefully. She knew Flynn needed to broaden his circle of acquaintances. And Michael was one of the nicest people she knew.

"He was all right," Flynn replied.

Cindy took a deep breath, remembering that men didn't verbalize their feelings, that Flynn had probably revealed all that was masculinely possible. "He and Katherine have been my anchors since I came to Rosewood. They're good friends to have."

"Hmmm."

She sighed inwardly. "I mean they could be good friends for you, too, Flynn."

"I'm not especially looking for a wild social whirl."

For a moment the past hung between them, the gregarious, fun-loving social circle they'd once traveled in, the one that had brought the Thompson sisters together with Flynn. Cindy fiddled with a bluebonnet she'd plucked from the grass. "No, but everyone needs friends."

"I don't need to borrow yours."

She wondered if it was Julia's death alone that had created such intense barriers. "They're not trinkets to be lent. One of the best things about a small town is getting to truly know people."

"But it seems most of the ones you know are connected with the church."

She frowned. "And that's so bad?"

"It's not for me."

"Have you considered getting to know them before judging their value as friends?"

The negative motion of his head was reluctant. "Cindy, I appreciate all you've done for the girls . . . for me. But like the office, or sending Michael Carlson, it's not necessary. You're doing too much already. I'm used to calling my own shots."

Unwanted compassion shadowed her thoughts and her voice. "But isn't that a lonely way to live?"

He raised his brows. "Seems I could ask you the same thing. After all, you moved to a town where you knew only one person, and you live alone in a house big enough for a huge family. Doesn't that seem a bit lonely to you?"

Pain, both past and present, assaulted

her. He would never know just how lonely she'd been. How difficult her life had been since he'd pilfered her heart. And meeting his eyes, she wondered how she could continue hiding that from him.

Chapter Five

†

By Sunday morning, however, Cindy was ready to put that aside. She'd invited Flynn to attend services with her, but he had curtly refused. She had nearly expected the same response when she told him she wanted to take the girls. He'd hesitated, but finally agreed, telling her the social part of Sunday school probably wouldn't hurt as long as she didn't fill the girls' heads with unrealistic ideas. In her opinion, nothing taught at her church was unrealistic, so she took him at his word.

And she chose to ignore the look on Flynn's face when they left. One that said this, too, was simply a fad Cindy would outgrow.

The girls loved Cindy's classic bright red convertible Mustang. Since she had left their curls loose and free, she didn't care that the breeze mussed their soft hair.

"What's at church?" Beth asked.

"That's where we go to learn about God and Jesus."

"Daddy says there's no God," Beth replied innocently.

Still the pain shot straight to Cindy's

heart. There was no easy answer, none she could offer that wouldn't confuse Beth. "Not everyone believes the same way, sweetie. As you get older, you'll learn about lots of new things."

"Is God new?" Beth asked.

Cindy smiled despite the pain still squeezing her heart. "No. He's older than the sky and the grass and the flowers and the trees."

"Is He older than Daddy?"

Another trickle of amusement sprouted at the child's guileless words. "Sure is."

"Real old, huh?"

"Yes, sweetie. Real old."

When they arrived at church, Cindy felt the welcoming fellowship like a balm to the wound that was Flynn.

Once the girls were happily ensconced in their class, Cindy was awfully glad she'd insisted on bringing them, despite Flynn's reservations. Again she remembered the look on his face any time she mentioned church. The man knew so little about her, it was pitiable.

It came as no surprise to Cindy that the triplets charmed everyone with their identical heart-shaped faces. It was difficult to withstand twins, impossible to resist triplets. Luckily, they were too young to let all the fawning go to their heads.

Katherine popped into the classroom, her eyes lighting up when she saw Cindy and the girls. Crossing to Cindy's side, she lowered her voice. "So you were able to make off with them?"

Cindy nodded, her brows raised in a matching mock conspiratorial motion. "It wasn't exactly the great heist, but I'm happy they're here."

"Any chance Daddy will be joining them?"

Cindy shook her head.

"Has he just fallen out of the habit?"

"I'm afraid it's much more than a broken habit."

"It isn't an unbreachable problem," Katherine reminded her, alluding to her husband's once-lost faith.

"I'm glad it worked out for you and Michael, but I don't know about Flynn. . . ."

"I wasn't certain at first about Michael, either."

Cindy's smile was bleak. "It's not as though this is a break in our relationship. We don't have a relationship to crater."

"I'm afraid you're focusing only on the big picture."

"In what way?"

"I think you need to take it one day at a

time. See what unfolds. Learn if Flynn realizes you're no longer a frivolous twenty-one-year-old. You told me that you've scarcely seen Flynn since he married your sister. To be fair, he hasn't had a chance to learn about the real you. Instead, you're an inaccurate memory. Don't you think it's time he got to know the real Cindy? While you're at it, subtly find out if he's in a crisis of faith, which calls for prayer, rather than worry."

Cindy looked at her friend whom she knew to be both caring and wise. "I haven't really thought about it that way. Maybe he's not as sure as he thinks he is."

"Sometimes we're so overwhelmed, we can't see the pieces as they separate and change."

"You know what, Katie-cakes?"

Katherine's grin erupted. "What?"

"I think you're in the right job."

Eyes rolling, Katherine hugged her lightly. "And you, my friend, are on the right track."

Maybe not yet, Cindy realized. But tomorrow was another chance, one she could use to apply Katherine's advice. And she was nothing if not tenacious.

The drive to Houston the following day

seemed longer than Flynn remembered. But perhaps that was because Cindy was at his side. He took another glance at her bright red dress, saucy hat and delicate high-heeled sandals. Hardly the outfit he'd expected her to choose for a board meeting. But then, when had Cindy ever done the expected? "You sure that Katherine will be all right taking care of the girls today?"

Cindy didn't disguise her sigh. "She knows it's for a good reason. Her calendar is clear, and to quote her, 'How can I possibly repay you for baby-sitting my children dozens and dozens of times?' It's not as though we have a meeting every day, or even every week. It's only once a month."

Flynn thought about the shares he'd inherited from Julia — half the stock in their family oil business. Ironically, it made he and Cindy unlikely partners, even though he'd ignored his inheritance until now. There had been no time — and it had been too painful a reminder. But Cindy had been insistent about attending the meeting. "Do we have to do much today?"

She shook her head. "Nope. The management staff has been in place for years, they know exactly what they're doing and we're just there to listen and vote if necessary."

He looked at her curiously. "I would think you'd care more about your family's business."

"Did you ever feel that way about Julia's participation?"

Nonplussed, he hesitated. "Well, no. But she — I mean you —"

"What you mean is that Julia had a purpose in her life that you don't see in mine, therefore she was excused. It happens that I chose to focus my life in a different direction."

One of fun and frolic. Just as she had when he'd met her. All motion and energy, but no substance. A flibbertigibbet, his late grandmother would have called her. "It's not up to me to judge your decisions."

Her eyes clouded. "No. But that doesn't stop you, does it?"

He held up one hand. "How about a truce for today? We can enjoy the big city — have lunch at a five-star restaurant without worrying that we'll be wearing half of it courtesy of the triplets."

She relented. "I suppose you're right. I usually do a little shopping while I'm in the city, too."

Flynn grimaced.

Cindy's laughter filled the closed space of the car. "Typical male reaction. I thought we could at least pick up something for the girls."

It was his turn to relent. "I suppose so."

Reaching downtown Houston, Flynn concentrated on the traffic-filled streets. "Gets worse every day."

"I don't know. I find all the people invigorating."

Despite the distraction of tall buildings and hordes of pedestrians, he turned to stare at her. "Yet you moved to Rosewood?"

"Mmm," she murmured.

And she didn't reveal much more as they parked, then attended the meeting. It was only afterward that she brightened again, suggesting they go to the Galleria for their shopping excursion.

FAO Schwarz was a child's fantasy. And Cindy seemed much like a child herself as she oohed and ahhed over the treasures the store contained. She agonized over the selection of three unique stuffed toys.

"Don't you want them to match?" Flynn asked.

She shook her head. "I've never taken to the notion that twins and triplets should be treated as a unit. It's fun to dress them identically at times, but they have to know they're individuals, with different tastes, dreams." Cindy reached for a stuffed bunny, still unable to decide.

"Aren't you going to get one for your-self?" he couldn't resist asking, seeing how absorbed she was in the task.

An unexpected tinge of color warmed her cheeks. "I do have a weakness for them, but I'll resist this once."

Funny, he thought she would indulge her least whim. Maybe she was having an off day.

But the thought had barely faded when she started looking at more toys.

"Actually, I don't want to spoil the girls," he told her. "It's great that you want to be generous, but I think we've gotten enough things for them."

She picked up the stuffed bunny she'd discarded a few moments earlier. "These aren't for the girls."

Once a playgirl, always a playgirl. Flynn was amazed that a woman of Cindy's age would want the bunny. But then her indulgences weren't his concern. Still, he felt a flash of remembered disappointment. One that was reminiscent of their first meeting. He'd seen the promise in her eyes, and had felt the disappointment of learning she was as scattered as Julia was collected.

With their purchases tucked safely in the trunk, Cindy talked him into an exotic restaurant that boasted only the unusual. She had promised to forgo granola and vegetarian fare, but he wasn't sure this was much better.

"So, what do you think?" she asked, excitement deepening the green of her eyes.

"Let me put it this way. I don't recall ever finding myself torn between ostrich and buffalo as my only possible entrée choices."

Her face, bright and mischievous, only sparkled more. "Great, isn't it? I mean any place can offer steak or fish."

Flynn had a sudden longing for just that banality. "So they could." He turned the menu over, glancing at the back. "I don't suppose they have pasta."

She rolled her eyes. "We had pasta for dinner last night."

"True. And what are the chances of finding spinach-and-wheat pasta twice in a row?"

Some of the pleasure in her expression dimmed. "Oh."

He swallowed a sigh. "Most pasta doesn't have that much flavor."

But her former sparkle had disappeared. "That's diplomatic."

"It really was good," he insisted. "I'm not used to a pine nut sauce, but the noodle part was good."

Unexpectedly she laughed. "We really should have gone to a steak place, shouldn't we? It's not too late. We haven't ordered yet."

"No. This is fine. How many chances will I have to try exotic meats?"

"If you stay at my house long enough, you might be surprised."

His actual surprise was the grin he found pushing his lips upward. "So, what do you recommend? Which delicacy won't we be trying?"

She took pity on him. "Both the buffalo and ostrich taste like beef, just a touch milder. And they're lower in fat, cholesterol and calories."

"It must work," he admitted.

Puzzled, she tilted her head. "What do you mean?"

"You're still turning heads, and none of the calories are sticking."

When she didn't immediately reply, he glanced up from the menu. But instead of a warm blush or sly demur, she had paled. "Something wrong?"

Cindy shook her head a bit too quickly and forcefully. "No. Just hungry. I didn't have any breakfast."

Flynn wasn't sure why, but he was certain that wasn't the truth. Still, he didn't argue the point; instead he listened as Cindy asked the waiter for a bowl of soup. He played along deliberately, sensing whatever was bothering her would only be exacerbated by anything else he could say.

It was unusual for Cindy. She normally steamed ahead with unrestricted fervor, energy and an undue need for control. But she never seemed weak.

And it affected him with unexpected emotion. Cindy had never struck him as needing protection.

As he watched, she pushed at the roll on her plate, but never picked it up. So it wasn't hunger. He wondered what it could be, what had so thoroughly shaken her. But throughout the meal she didn't meet his eyes.

And that made him want to know all the more.

A few days later Cindy tucked the new toys into place in the Rainbow classroom. She had chosen each one with a particular child in mind, and she could just picture their faces when they came to the next session.

"Hey, you," Katherine greeted her, strolling into the room. "I thought I saw the light on in here."

"Just getting things ready for tomorrow."

Katherine glanced around the empty room. "And where are your three new appendages?"

Cindy smiled, but her heart wasn't in the effort. "Flynn has them. I think he believes I'd like to take them over."

Katherine's smile was wise, knowing. "Wouldn't you?"

"Absolutely. But not away from him. And Flynn has this all-or-nothing mentality."

"I don't suppose you've considered the possibility that he thinks you might need a break from their constant care?"

Cindy furrowed her brow as she sank into one of the kid-size chairs. "No."

"It's not a competition," Katherine reminded her gently.

"I don't look at it that way!"

"Not even a little bit?"

Deflated, Cindy stared at her friend, the only one who knew her secrets and still didn't judge her. "I suppose I do feel I have a lot to prove."

"Do you remember when I was agonizing about Michael? Trying to change myself into the woman I thought he wanted?"

Cindy nodded.

"And do you remember what you told me? That if he didn't love me for myself, he wasn't the right one for me?"

"All too well," Cindy admitted. "I guess that's the crux of it. I don't really want to change for him, yet I suppose I hoped he'd see me in a new light, realize my value."

"If he doesn't, then he's blind."

Cindy's smile struggled to form, but failed. "Don't you see? He always has been as far as I've been concerned. After he took one look at Julia, I was as appealing as an Easter egg you find in the middle of the summer."

Katherine couldn't stifle a smile. "Oh, Cindy. How can he not see how special you are? How much joy and adventure you bring to everything?"

Cindy shrugged. "He doesn't care for adventure — that's why he chose Julia."

Wincing for her friend, Katherine met Cindy's gaze, her voice gentle. "You also told me that I couldn't be a substitute."

"Believe it or not, that's been the foremost thing on my mind these days. Even if I never find another man to love the way I do Flynn, I won't settle for being Julia's substitute."

"I suspected as much." Katherine hesitated. "Do you suppose now that Flynn is here, some of the illusion of denied love will lose its appeal?"

Cindy couldn't control the tears that spurted, or the trembling of her lips. "That's just it. Now that he's here, it's just worse. I don't know why. I can't explain it. There is something about Flynn and only Flynn that's in my heart and won't go away. I've tried, Kath, I really have." The tears gave way to gulping sobs. "I've tried not to love him, but it's still there, every moment of every day."

Katherine reached out, enveloping her in a hug, one that vibrated with great shaking wails of pain. And one that Cindy was helpless to stop.

That same evening Flynn tried to keep the lid on the rice cooker, while making sure the girls didn't tug on any of the pot handles on the stove. But that was harder than he'd expected. Fearing they'd pull a pot off and burn themselves, he put them in the next room with a children's video.

He'd chopped and diced for what seemed like hours. He'd found a fairly palatable-sounding recipe in one of Cindy's cookbooks. It was a tofu stir-fry seasoned with oyster sauce. The instructions promised that the tofu would then taste like oysters. He had his doubts, but the dinner he was preparing wasn't for him. It was for Cindy.

Belatedly it had occurred to him that perhaps she was worn-out. She still kept up her hectic social schedule with her Rainbow thing as well as other functions, and she'd also assumed the majority of the triplets' care. Cooking dinner wouldn't make a big dent in that pressure, but maybe it would create a small vent. The girls had loved going shopping for the ingredients. But some of their suggestions had the stir-fry looking a little questionable.

"What's going on?" Cindy asked from the doorway.

Flynn spun around, seeing her gaze take in the messy kitchen. "You're early. I'd planned to have everything cleaned up before you got here."

"Oh," she answered in a small voice.

"But I did get the table set in the dining room."

"The dining room?" she echoed.

"Yeah. The stir-fry should be done soon."

"You're making stir-fry?"

He held up the cookbook. "I found the recipe in here. Between the grocery and health food stores we found everything we needed."

"That's what you were doing today?"

He smiled. "As you pointed out, there's

not a lot of action in Rosewood. And the girls enjoyed it."

"Well . . ."

"I'd planned to have it all arranged in the dining room, but . . . surprise!"

"Surprise?" she echoed, looking stunned.

"Yeah. To say thanks for all you do for me, for the girls." He walked toward the small sitting room just off the kitchen. "Girls, Cindy's home." As they scampered toward him, he stopped Alice, whispering to her, "Get your surprise."

In a few moments Alice returned and came toward Cindy with a bouquet of daisies.

Cindy's eyes misted as she accepted the flowers, then gave Alice a fierce hug.

"They seemed to suit you," Flynn explained. "The daisies, I mean."

Cindy's throat worked. But Beth and Mandy were rushing at her, as well. Scooping them up in a hug, she hid her face behind their compact bodies. And Flynn couldn't help wondering what was going on in that fiery head of hers.

Finally her face emerged as she settled the girls back on to the floor. "This is really nice. The dinner —" she held up the bouquet "— the flowers. Thanks."

"I don't say it often enough, but you've

changed our lives and we appreciate it."

Remarkably he thought her eyes brightened with the suspicion of tears. But that couldn't be. Not freewheeling Cindy. She was all laughter, not tears.

She lowered her face, presumably to sniff the daisies. Her voice was soft, nearly muffled. "And you have changed mine."

The girls pulled at her hands, tugging her toward the dining room to show off the table setting. But Flynn didn't follow, instead remembering the remarkable look on her face, the remembered feelings it evoked. Feelings he thought he'd put to rest the day he proposed to Julia.

Chapter Six

†

A few days later, Flynn entered his daughters' room. Once again he admired all of Cindy's handiwork, but still he felt she had gone overboard. She claimed she wasn't spoiling the girls, but he was worried about all her overly generous gestures. From experience he knew it wasn't wise to grow up believing life was always this kind.

He reached down to pick up a discarded pair of pajamas the girls had left behind. As he stood, he noticed a new addition to the room. A picture of Jesus.

All the betrayal of his past choked him. It was one thing to spoil the girls, it was another to tamper with their beliefs.

Hearing Cindy's steps in the hall outside the room, he called out for her. "Would you come in here?"

The echo of footfalls on the wooden floor paused, then turned into the room. "Yes?"

"What's this?"

She glanced around the room. "What?"

"Don't play games. This picture."

Cindy looked back at him wryly. "Well, I

think that's pretty obvious."

"What's it doing in here?"

She pointed to another picture on the wall — one filled with cartoon characters. "I'm decorating their room."

"The picture of Jesus isn't a decoration. It's a statement."

"I think that's an exaggeration. The girls aren't even three years old yet."

"The younger the mind, the easier it is to brainwash."

"*Brainwash?*"

"Influence, then."

"Flynn, they're babies!"

"Then why the picture of Jesus?"

She hedged for only a moment. "I like the idea of Him looking over them, protecting them."

"That's a fairy tale," he told her flatly, deep anger and remembered pain darkening his thoughts.

Shocked, she stared at him. "You can't mean that!"

"Don't delude yourself, Cindy. Especially for a craze you'll forget by next month."

Hurt flashed in her eyes. "Is that what you think of me? That I'm chasing fads like a teenager?"

Exasperated, unwilling to face the pain in her expression, he threw up his hands. "All I asked is a simple question."

"Then I'll give you a *simple* answer. Your lack of faith is going to hurt your daughters. If you're having a crisis of faith —"

"You don't know what you're talking about," he responded, with only the slightest grip on his anger.

She studied him, opened her mouth, then closed it again. Nodding, she turned away.

"Cindy?"

She glanced at the picture on the wall. "I'll take it down later. But I can't guarantee that you won't see it somewhere else in the house."

Unable to watch her leave, he turned toward the window. Then he heard the sound of tiny steps, then a tug on his jeans.

Flynn glanced down. "Hey there, Alice."

"Up?" she asked.

He obliged, picking her up until they were at eye level.

"Daddy?"

"Yes, sweetie."

"Why you hate Jesus?"

He hadn't known a fist to the gut could be delivered by a guileless toddler. "What makes you say that?"

Alice screwed up her precious face. "Me heard fight with Cinny. I wanna have Jesus here."

"But it's only a picture."

"How come, then?"

Why not indeed? It was only a picture, it had no power over them. Over him.

Yet the torturous question accompanied him as he went through the motions of the day. It was late afternoon when he finally sought Cindy out again.

She was in the kitchen, preparing a huge casserole.

"That's quite a lot of food," he commented, not certain how to begin this discussion.

"For tonight," Cindy replied. Then she glanced up, catching his puzzled glance. "Remember the people coming over tonight? I told you about them."

"Oh, right. I'll clear out pretty soon."

Exasperation flooded her expression. "Flynn. I invited them over to meet you."

He'd completely forgotten, caught up in hours of rare contemplation, a prisoner of a past he'd never outrun. "Of course."

A buzzer went off and she walked to the oven, pulling out a fragrant tray of rolls. Searching for a place to put them on the crowded tile counter, she glanced up at him. "Did you need something?"

He moved aside the casserole dish at the end of the counter, making a place for the rolls. "I've been thinking . . . ."

Uncharacteristically, she didn't jump in with words to ease his way.

Which made him feel even stiffer, more uncomfortable. "It's about this morning . . . the picture. You can leave it in their room."

She studied him silently, again surprising him. Flynn wondered where all her fiery words had gone. Especially when she only nodded.

He considered an apology, but the place inside him that held those words had been dammed up long ago. "Do you need any help?"

She seemed to consider this, too. Then she gestured toward the fridge. "You could put the salad together."

"Sprouts included?"

But her usual ready laughter didn't surface. "Whatever you'd like to put in it. The vegetable drawer is pretty full."

They worked in silence for a while. Flynn wasn't certain how to break the strain, how to bring the sparkle and laughter back to Cindy's face.

She glanced up at the clock. "Yipes, I still have to shower and change my clothes before everyone gets here."

"I can finish in here," he offered, surprising himself as much as Cindy.

"Well, I did want to tidy up —"

114

"I can take care of it," he insisted.

She took a final glance at the food, then nodded. "The table's set and —"

"Go."

"And I —"

"Go."

And she did.

It didn't take long to clean up the kitchen, then check on the girls who were making Play-Doh teddy bears on the faded, terrazzo terrace. Because of the tall, wide windows he'd been able to watch them as Cindy had been doing before he arrived.

He remembered the first time he'd tried to feed the girls and clean up while watching them. It had never occurred to him to put them in the safety of the fenced backyard. An old wooden toy box beneath the awning held a large and varied collection of toys to keep them occupied.

His daughters looked content, having assimilated into Cindy's life and home as though they'd always been here. He thought of the gathering Cindy had planned for the evening, suspecting she hoped to accomplish the same for him. Knowing that hadn't been possible since he was a child, equally certain it would never be possible again.

There was something about a group of

people who'd known each other long and well. Their chatter filled the air, snatches of conversation that melded from person to person. It seemed everyone was talking at once, but in a good way. No one was excluded, no one hanging outside the fringes of the group.

And due to Cindy, Flynn was included, as well. She'd introduced him to the collection of people who ranged greatly in age and background. Ruth Stanton, a perky seventy-two-year-old woman, welcomed Flynn as warmly as did people of his own age, and some much younger.

Having met Michael and Katherine Carlson before, Flynn felt a little more comfortable with them. Michael in turn introduced him to Tom Sanders, clearly a good friend, also a casual, warm person. Then he met Gregg Rosentreter, Roger Dalton, Don Westien and Gary Simpson. All the men, obviously good friends, were welcoming.

The fact that it seemed everyone at the party attended Rosewood Community Church wasn't lost on Flynn.

Seeing Cindy heading toward the kitchen, Flynn followed her, relieved to see no one else was in the room. "How'd you go about assembling the guest list for tonight?"

She thought for a moment. "Well, you'd

met Michael and seemed to like him. I thought you might have something in common with the other guys he's friends with — also, they're people I especially like."

"No other motive?"

Frowning, she narrowed her eyes. "Such as?"

"They all go to your church."

She relaxed a fraction. "That's where I met my friends."

"*All* of your friends go to your church?"

A touch of exasperation entered her expression. "It's not a requirement. I'm friends with some of my neighbors, other people I've met in town. But, yes, my closest friends are those from the church. You'll notice I did invite most of the people who live on this street, as well."

"To throw me off the scent?"

Something flickered in her green eyes, a flash she quickly disguised. "The sole purpose of tonight's party is to introduce you to people in the town you've chosen to call home. I'm sorry it bothers you that so many of them attend my church. But I could hardly walk the streets and invite total strangers."

Looking at her, the evidence of her temperament, as fiery as her hair, challenged him. Again, he couldn't help comparing her to Julia, remembering how his late wife would never have confronted him. "No, I don't suppose you could. Cindy, I do appreciate your effort but —"

"You didn't ask for a party. I know. Just me being me again."

"Cindy —"

The tall swinging door pushed open. "Here you are," Katherine exclaimed. "Can I help do anything?"

Flynn watched as Cindy reluctantly pulled her gaze away. "Yes," Cindy replied shortly. "Keep Flynn entertained. I'll take some more punch into the dining room." The door swung smartly behind Cindy as she exited.

Uncomfortably Flynn studied Katherine, wondering if he was about to get a sermon.

Katherine strolled over to the oven, opening it to peek inside. "Cindy makes killer crab puffs."

"Pardon me?"

"Her crab puffs — they're great. I know she's into granola and nuts, but she can cook up a storm of gooey, good stuff when she wants to."

"Oh. Well, we've gotten used to her cooking."

Katherine laughed. "Better you than me.

118

When she and I go out, I pick the restaurant and you should see her put away a hamburger and shake."

Flynn suspected Katherine wanted to talk about more than food, yet he stuck to the safety of the subject. "The main course tonight is vegetable lasagna."

"Now that's one of her healthy creations I love." Katherine closed the oven door. "But that's our Cindy, a mass of contradictions."

He should have escaped right after the crab puff remark. Now he was stuck. "Yeah, I suppose so."

"How many trust fund kids do you know who devote their lives to volunteer work instead of shopping and gliding around the world?"

Flynn stiffened. Apparently Katherine didn't know her friend as well as she thought. "For the time being, anyway."

But Katherine didn't immediately rebut the reply. "So, that's how it is."

"Excuse me?"

"Nothing. I'm glad you and your daughters are getting settled in."

"Well, we will when my house is finished."

"Of course. It's always difficult to blend two lives."

Flynn remained cautious. "Cindy's been

patient, but we're intruding on her routine."

Katherine shrugged. "I haven't heard that from her. It's a difficult time for you and your daughters and I know she's thrilled to be able to help out. But you know Cindy, she just wishes she could do more."

Flynn studied her, wondering at any hidden meaning. "I'm not sure what that would be."

Katherine's smile, however, was enigmatic. "She probably doesn't, either."

The kitchen door was pushed open again. Without looking at Flynn, Cindy walked over to the oven.

"They looked almost done when I checked them," Katherine offered.

"Thanks."

Katherine nodded, then left the room.

The remaining silence was a palpable thing.

Flynn felt forced to end it. "Katherine says you make killer crab puffs."

"Yeah, well, Katherine tends to be a bit prejudiced." Cindy withdrew the baking sheet, transferring the appetizers to a porcelain tray. "We'd better get back in there."

"Cindy?"

She didn't meet his eyes. "Yes?"

"I seem to have a way of irritating you on

120

a daily basis. I guess I'm just not used to someone taking control of things, offering so much. It was really great of you to arrange this party tonight."

This time, she did raise her eyes, her green eyes darkened to the color of sheltered, unlit forests. "So what else is new? I'll never be like Julia and everything I do is a daily reminder of that."

"That's not what I meant."

Cindy walked toward the door, one hand on the old wood, prepared to push it open. "Yes, it is. Even if you don't want to admit it."

Flynn followed her slowly. Why did Cindy think he would want her to behave as Julia had? Julia was his wife and Cindy was . . . Cindy.

Walking into the crowded parlor, he was immediately swept into the group of people. Michael made a point of including him in his conversation with Tom Sanders.

It was a friendly gathering. Everyone seemed genuine, most made hospitable offers ranging from baby-sitting services to help on the house he was building. It was rather amazing.

"We start softball practice this Saturday," Michael was telling him.

"I'm not sure I have time to —"

121

"We don't take no for an answer. Just ask Michael," Tom Sanders added.

Michael's grin was wry. "I can vouch for that. It's a lot of fun. And we can always use another player."

Flynn looked from one determined face to the other. "Why don't we see how Saturday shapes up? I don't want to dump the kids on Cindy for the day."

"Are you kidding?" Tom asked. "She's nuts about your girls."

Puzzled Flynn stared at him. "And you know that . . . how?"

"She talks about them constantly," Tom replied. "She's as proud of them as any parent."

Unconsciously Flynn stiffened. "She's their *aunt*."

Tom shrugged. "I wish I'd had an aunt like Cindy, someone who makes everything seem like a treat. I think Cindy could make fun out of a pile of sticks in the rain."

Flynn studied Tom, wondering if the man had more than friendly feelings for Cindy. "So, you and your wife have been friends with her for a while now?"

"I'm not married," Tom replied. "Not anymore."

Which meant he and Cindy could well be more than friends. Funny, he didn't seem like her type. Flynn shook away the thought. It wasn't any of his business whom Cindy chose to date. Yet he found himself observing Tom, evaluating the other man.

As the evening drew to a close, all the departing male guests reminded Flynn of the upcoming weekend softball game. And, oddly, he was tempted to go.

When the door closed behind their last guest, Flynn watched as Cindy began to quietly collect bowls and trays. He joined her, filling his hands with the delicate china Cindy treasured. "So what do you think about their insistence that I play softball?"

"I think you should do what you want to."

Flynn angled his head. "That doesn't sound like you."

She turned briefly. "How would you know?"

"What?"

"You don't know me at all. How could you possibly think you would recognize when I'm being myself?" Not waiting for an answer, she disappeared into the kitchen.

Flynn was left holding the delicate china, as deceptively fragile, it seemed, as Cindy herself.

The softball field was much like Rosewood itself, old-fashioned and appealing. A small shack sold ice-cream cones, canned soda and homemade hot dogs.

Cindy made sure the triplets held hands, an uneven line of rambunctious little bodies. She'd been surprised that Flynn had agreed to come to this first practice. Reluctant to the point of reticence, she had expected him to find a thousand excuses not to go.

She wondered if Michael's unscheduled, unexpected visit the previous night had made a difference. Busy with the triplets, she hadn't heard their discussion. And then this morning, Flynn had announced his intention to attend the game.

Seeing her friend, Cindy waved at Katherine, who waved back while angling her head in Flynn's direction.

No need to be subtle, Cindy wanted to shout. But Flynn hadn't seemed to notice. Relieved, she walked the girls around the small field.

Tom approached with a grin. "So, how are the four most beautiful women in town?"

Cindy winked, recognizing Tom's harmless teasing.

He responded by tugging her pert ponytail, making the girls giggle.

Since Tom was much like a brother, she

only shook her head in bemusement.

He knelt down, bringing his gaze eye level with the triplets. "So. You going to clap and cheer for Daddy or for me?"

"Daddy!" they chorused loyally.

He whistled. "Tough crowd." Standing back up, Tom reached for Cindy's cooler. "I'll carry this over to the bleachers."

"Thanks. That gives me at least one free hand."

"Cute kids, Cindy."

"Yeah, they really are."

Tom glanced down, seeing that the girls weren't paying attention. "Lucky break Flynn decided to move to Rosewood."

Cindy withheld the sigh that had been building inside since Flynn's first mention of relocation. "Yeah, lucky."

Tom slowed his steps. "Everything okay, Cin?"

She met his concerned gaze. "I finally have some family here. It's spring. What could be wrong?"

He hooked his arm with her free one. "Remember, you can tell me if something's wrong. I have a sturdy shoulder."

She glanced up at him with a heartfelt smile. "So you do."

"Cindy?" Flynn snagged her attention.

Startled, she glanced at him, not aware

125

he'd walked over to their little group. "Yes?"

He glanced at her arm, still loosely linked with Tom's. "Are you sure you can handle all the girls by yourself?"

Tom discreetly dropped her arm and self-consciously she pushed at the hair that fell across her forehead. "Of course. Why?"

Flynn glanced once again at Tom. "They can be a handful."

She shrugged. "I brought treats." She motioned with her head to the swing set, slide and seesaw in the park beside the softball field. "And there's plenty to keep them busy. Besides, they can't wait to see you play."

"Daddy play!" Beth demanded.

Flynn scooped her up. "In a few minutes."

Mandy tugged at his pants leg, as well, but Alice hung on to Cindy's hand. Flynn obliged by picking up Mandy, giving both girls a hug, then putting them back down.

"We have to let Daddy go practice," Cindy explained.

"Me play, too," Beth demanded.

"No," Cindy told her firmly. "This is Daddy's day."

"She could walk to the field with me for a

few minutes," Flynn replied.

Cindy wanted to thump him. And he thought *she* was spoiling them? "I spent quite a bit of time explaining to the girls that this is a grown-up game, that little girls don't get to play."

"I didn't intend to let her play."

"No, but I'll spend the entire time keeping her off the field if you take her out there."

"That's an exaggeration," Flynn replied.

Tom cleared his throat. "I'd better get back to the practice." He held up the cooler. "I'll put this on the bleachers."

"Thanks," Cindy replied, wondering why Flynn was scowling as though he had ants in his shoes.

"Sure," Tom replied, walking away quickly.

"What's with you?" Cindy asked.

Flynn's scowl didn't lighten. "Problem?"

"You just chased away one of the nicest people here. Some special reason why?"

"You tell me."

Puzzled, Cindy grasped Alice's hand a little tighter. "So, are we going to grapple over taking the girls on the field?"

He looked at her for a long moment. "No, I don't guess we will."

Then his gaze shifted toward Tom.

"Nothing to argue about at all."

Confused, Cindy stared after him as he stalked on to the field. And for the life of her, she couldn't imagine why he hadn't taken to Tom.

"Men," she muttered.

"Men?" Beth asked.

"Yes, sweetie. We'll talk more about them when you're older. For now we'll stick to Cinderella and Prince Charming."

Mandy drew her brows together. "Like Daddy?"

Yep. However, Cindy was the only girl in the world whose glass slipper wouldn't fit. At least not for Prince Flynn.

Chapter Seven

†

Two mornings later, Cindy carefully banded the remaining stacks of paper, making certain each was straight and in order. She glanced down at the three nearly filled cardboard boxes, then back at the almost bare desktop.

It didn't take a crystal ball to know that Flynn wouldn't appreciate the fact that she'd packed everything without consulting him. But a late-night phone call had taken precedence over Flynn's makeshift office.

Her Rainbow class, already strained by growing pains, had suddenly acquired six new members. And even Cindy, who possessed an inordinate amount of energy, knew she didn't have enough stamina to spread that thinly. The only solution was to cut the class in half so they would be manageable groups. That meant two different meeting times.

And they had run out of space at the church. Rosewood Community had begun a small private academy in the Sunday school building the last year, and they already needed the space allotted to Cindy's

129

Rainbow class. Obtaining it for an additional day each week wasn't possible.

As her class had grown, she and Katherine had discussed the necessity of relocating the Rainbow group. That's when Cindy had handpicked her own conservatory for the purpose. Then Flynn had needed an office and she'd been able to put off the move. But now there was no other choice. Her parlor, with all its breakable collectibles wasn't suitable. And she couldn't keep the kids in the yard the entire time.

"Hey, what's going on?" Flynn demanded from the doorway, his sleep-tousled hair still a bit wild.

Cindy glanced up, immediately assessing his displeasure. "I need to use this room for my Rainbow class."

He frowned. "So you're just clearing out my stuff?"

"You *did* tell me you wanted to handle your own office arrangements, in fact all your arrangements."

He gestured to the boxes. "Is this what you call allowing me to handle my own decisions? Packing my things without consulting me?"

She rolled her eyes. "Do you want me to remind you how often you've mentioned that you'd prefer the office space you rented to this one?"

"One small point — it's not ready yet."

Cindy shrugged. "Michael offered to help. But you wouldn't even let him make a phone call. If you had, maybe the space would be finished by now."

"I don't impose on strangers."

"Michael's not a stranger!"

"Not to you. I barely know him."

Exasperated, she tossed down a manila folder. "By your choice. My friends have extended themselves, but you purposely remain distant."

"Another thing I don't believe I asked for," he reminded her in a tight voice.

She leaned back against the desk. "Look, Flynn. I don't know how things were done with your friends. But in a small town like Rosewood, we depend on each other and our faith."

"One more strike and you're out."

Dismayed, she stared at him. "I still can't believe you mean that."

Impatiently he smoothed one hand back over his chestnut hair. "And you accused *me* of ignoring what I didn't want to hear?"

She fiddled for a moment with the deep blue antique glass inkwell. "I hate to think of you having such a gaping hole in your life, one nothing else can fill."

"And I hate to think I'm going to have to endure a sermon. If I'm going to move today, I'd better get to it."

But she didn't stir, instead raising her eyes. "I wouldn't have put you out of your office if it wasn't for a good cause. My Rainbow class has nearly doubled and there's no other space available."

Flynn muttered under his breath.

Cindy couldn't distinguish the words, but suspected she wouldn't want to hear them if she could. Turning around, she scribbled on a notepad, then ripped the page free. "We can still call Michael about your office."

"How about if you let me make that *one* decision?"

"Of course." She handed him the paper. "Here's his number." She took one more step toward the door, then hesitated. "I know you think I want to wrestle away your control. But it's never been about that. I feel how much pain you've been in since you lost Julia, then all the responsibility of raising the girls on your own. I was just trying to make things easier for you, to let you not have to worry for once."

Flynn stared at her, not replying.

And so she left him there, not certain

what he would have said if he'd spoken. Nearly as certain she wouldn't have wanted to hear the words.

Later that morning Flynn studied the bare, dusty space he'd rented. Not much had been accomplished since he'd examined it a week before. He bent to test one of the outlets. No current. He couldn't even plug in his laptop. The spot where the phone jack was to be installed was still a bare empty hole.

He sighed. He could run his computer off the batteries and depend on his cell phone, but it was hardly an ideal situation. And he was eager to set up the business that had been fermenting in his mind. Details were coming together daily, and he was having new development ideas on an almost hourly basis. He also needed to hire a few employees. Glancing around, he realized he couldn't expect anyone else to work alongside him in this disaster area.

Reluctantly he pulled the wadded-up piece of paper from his pocket. He stared from his cell phone to the number Cindy had scrawled. With equal hesitation he punched in the number.

Michael didn't seem to think it was odd that he'd waited so long to call, agreeing to stop by within the hour.

It was an unusually long hour for Flynn. He couldn't repress the memory of Cindy's face, the seeming sincerity of her words. What was it about her that seemed to be crawling under his skin? Admittedly in a way that had never before happened. Not even with Julia. Safe, unthreatening Julia.

And the realization made him want to run, fast and far. Then he pictured his daughters' precious faces. They adored "Cinny" and no amount of logic or reasoning could change that.

Still the minutes dawdled. It wasn't Michael, Flynn knew. It was his own past pushing at him. A familiar suffocating feeling gripped him and Flynn headed outside.

It was there that Michael found him, as he pulled into the parking lot. He had brought coffee for them both. Sipping from thick paper cups, they canvassed the area.

It didn't take long for Michael to make an assessment. "This should have been finished not too long after we talked the first time," he told Flynn bluntly.

"Can you recommend another contractor?" Flynn asked. "I know you work mainly on big projects, so —"

"I told you I do all sorts of construction.

I'd be happy to put a crew on it," Michael interrupted.

"But this is a piddling job compared to what you're probably accustomed to."

He shrugged. "You need an office. I have a crew."

Flynn narrowed his eyes. "Did Cindy call you?"

"No. Should she have?"

Flynn hesitated. "I'm not accustomed to accepting favors."

Michael grinned. "Don't worry. I'll send you a bill." He glanced at his watch. "How 'bout some lunch?"

"I don't want to tie up your entire afternoon."

"Gotta eat."

"Yeah," Flynn agreed. "So we do."

Rarely allowing himself to get close enough to form fast friendships, it surprised Flynn to find himself comfortable in Michael's company. But for once he didn't question it. Cindy had provided more than enough questions to chew on.

Many of the kids in the Rainbow class had been to Cindy's house before. And they were happy to return. She had set up projects in the conservatory, kitchen and on the terrace.

It rarely mattered to the children what tasks she chose. They simply enjoyed the nurturing and acceptance Cindy offered. Originally she had assumed that the boys wouldn't enjoy making cookies, but they had lined up alongside the girls at the big, oak table in the kitchen, eager to roll the dough and cut out shapes.

"I gotta horse!" young Ricky Dunn announced, holding up the sturdy dough.

Cindy couldn't contain a smile as she glimpsed his precocious grin and widened deep blue eyes. Although his shock of thick, dark hair needed to be trimmed, he looked perfect to her. This particular child had endured so much sadness in his young life, it was a thrill to see him excited over something as simple as a cookie. His father had died when Ricky was barely a year old. And his mother had been suffering from cancer for the last few years. Even someone as young as Ricky could see that his mother continued to look worse, rather than better. And just a year before, he had lost his only remaining grandparents in a freak accident when a pilot light was extinguished and they died in their sleep from the lethal, escaping gas. Now Ricky was alone in the world with only his fragile, ailing mother.

So Cindy was understanding when he

sometimes acted out, getting in one minor scrape after another. She sensed the fear behind the acts and offered him nurturing acceptance.

Now Ricky's comment had the others offering her views of their own cookies. She kept a huge old basket filled with cookie cutters, some from her own childhood and newer ones she'd purchased to fit even the smallest hands.

Allowing the kids to each pick one favorite cutter, she then encouraged them to trade and share with the others. So many of them desperately needed that social skill, one that wasn't easily acquired in their dysfunctional families.

"What in the world?" Flynn muttered from the hallway.

"Making cookies!" Beth chirped, still slathering sprinkles on her tiny, misshapen mound of dough.

Cindy glanced at Flynn's face, set in lines of surprised disapproval. "So, how'd the move to your office go?"

"Fine."

She thought it would be easier to pull the moisture from a year-old apple than words from Flynn at times. Holding in a sigh, she smiled instead. "We should have a batch done soon."

"Mmm," he replied.

"Oh, you don't know the kids." Cindy laid down the spatula she held, moving from child to child, resting her hands lightly on each one's shoulders as she introduced them to Flynn.

He greeted them kindly, yet Cindy could still sense his reserve. Seeing the questions in his eyes, she picked up a tray, motioning for Flynn to follow her into the dining room. When they were alone, she turned to him. "Shoot."

Lifting a brow at her directness, he spoke as bluntly as she had. "What's with all the kids? Some sort of charity play date?"

Cindy stiffened in automatic defense. "What's that supposed to mean?"

"A few of them look as though you picked them up at a shelter."

Mild fury blended with her protective instincts. "I didn't realize you were a clothing critic, as well."

He waved a hand in dismissal. "I'm guessing you just didn't know what you were getting yourself into."

"No, that's where you're wrong. I know *precisely* what I've taken on. Why do you suppose the Rainbow class is so important to me?"

His eyes widened in surprise. "*This* is

your Rainbow thing?"

She nodded.

Shock battled with disapproval in his expression. "Why didn't you tell me it was a kid class?"

She shrugged. "I assumed you knew. What did you think I was doing?"

"I don't know, pottery or some social thing."

Exasperation literally oozed from her pores. "You thought I'd run off the first day you were here, leaving you to deal with the girls on your own, for a *pottery* class?"

He shrugged. "It really wasn't any of my business."

Frustration fumed, but she couldn't spit out enough words to express it.

Flynn gestured toward the front of the house. "You told me you needed the conservatory. Yet you've filled the kitchen with kids."

"I need both," she explained with what little was left of her patience. "We do story and music time in the conservatory. And the floor's perfect for nap time."

"Music?" he questioned. "Are you hoping to produce another Mozart?"

She counted silently to ten. "Not necessarily. But I wouldn't dismiss the idea, either."

He frowned. "The piano's in your parlor and I haven't heard you play it since we've been here."

"I've been busy," she replied with a renewed touch of exasperation. "Besides, I also play the violin, guitar and mandolin. That's what we use in the conservatory."

Flynn studied her in surprise. "I didn't know you were musical."

She gritted her teeth against the rush of words begging to be spoken. "There's a lot you don't know about me, Flynn."

He glanced back toward the kitchen. "Why did you have to include the triplets in your charity project?"

She might thump him yet, Cindy realized. "I would appreciate you not referring to my Rainbow kids as a charity project. And why wouldn't I include the girls?"

"Well, by the look of some of those kids . . ."

A big mallet, she decided, one that would pound some sense into that thick head of his. "Are you saying my ragamuffins aren't good enough to play with your children?"

An unexpected look of shame flashed in his eyes, then was gone. "What do you know about them, Cindy? They could be the products of pretty unsavory backgrounds."

"Exactly, Flynn. That's why they need

me. Not every child has the luxury of loving parents and a father who can snap his fingers and produce every material need they could ever want."

Another sort of flush infused his face. "I worked hard for every penny I earned. I wasn't a trust fund baby who could play at will and still have a fortune at my disposal."

She felt the stab at his insult and instantly wondered if he'd ever said such a thing to Julia. "Yet you married a trust fund baby."

"You and Julia couldn't be more different if you'd been conceived on separate planets!"

That truth nearly took the breath from her. But she refused to let him know it. "Then, lucky you for picking the right sister. Now, if you don't mind, I have children to supervise." She stalked toward the doorway, pausing to glance back around. "And if you'd like to start teaching your daughters the value of snobbery and condescension, feel free to yank them out of the kitchen."

Three days later Flynn and Cindy were still tiptoeing around each other. Which made him glad that Cindy had taken back his temporary office.

Though he'd expected Michael to complete his space sooner than the previous contractor, he had been amazed by the skill and speed of his experienced crew.

Even now, Michael was checking over the last of the finishing work. "I think you should be set by the end of next week."

"That's great." Gratified, Flynn studied the other man. "How do you manage to oversee all the projects you've got going?"

"I don't," Michael admitted. "I used to try. Then I met Katherine. She convinced me that my children needed to be seen by me more often than a baby-sitter, so I hired a second-in-command. Now I choose the jobs I want to manage, and still have enough time for my family."

Puzzled, Flynn drew his brows together. "I must be missing something. That chronology doesn't work."

Michael nodded. "I guess no one told you. Katherine and I were married about two and a half years ago."

Flynn couldn't hide his surprise. "The way she treats them, I thought David and Annie were her children."

"Yeah. That's part of what makes her so special. Sounds hard to believe, but I honestly think she has the deepest feelings for our two oldest kids. Not that she isn't equally loving with the baby. But I guess she fell in love with David and Annie first."

Flynn considered a polite comment, then pushed it aside. "It's none of my business, but did you divorce or —"

"Like you, I lost my first wife. Never dreamed I'd ever marry again. And Katherine couldn't be any more different from Ruth." He shrugged. "Maybe that's why it works so well. I don't think I could have lived a life of comparisons, accumulating similarities instead of building a new life." Michael pushed his cap back. "I'm beginning to sound like a segment on *Oprah.*"

Unexpectedly Flynn laughed. "I've barely talked to anyone besides Cindy since I moved here, so it didn't even faze me."

"Whew," Michael replied. "Katherine and Cindy have a unique way of getting people to think along their wavelengths. But for some reason, I have a sudden need to watch a ball game or drive about a hundred nails in the wall."

Flynn thumbed his hand toward the nearly completed interior. "I doubt your crew would appreciate the gesture. I have a better idea. Why don't we get a card game together?" Then he stopped. "I forgot there for a moment that I don't have a house to offer."

"Cindy wouldn't care. But there's no

need. Mine's available. Katherine has a Mommy & Me thing planned for tonight. I can call the guys." He paused. "Guess you'd better make sure you have a sitter for the girls."

"Yeah," Flynn replied slowly, knowing he didn't want to ask the favor of Cindy.

"Why don't we say seven o'clock? Just call if there's a problem."

"Sure." Flynn pulled himself out of his thoughts. "And thanks for getting this place together so quickly."

"It's what I do."

The words had a familiar ring, but Flynn couldn't pinpoint them until hours later when he faced Cindy. They were almost identical to ones she had uttered earlier.

"Can you give me the names of a few baby-sitters you trust?" he asked, watching as she prepared shish kebabs made with chunky vegetables.

"Any special reason?" she asked.

"Michael Carlson's getting a card game together for tonight. I don't want to just dump the girls on you."

She paused, a metal skewer in one hand, a cherry tomato in the other. "Wasn't that the point of moving the Rosewood? So the girls wouldn't be left in the care of baby-sitters?"

"You're right. I can cancel the game."

She made an odd, strangulated sound. "I will be happy to watch the girls."

"You sure you don't have plans?"

She picked up a pearl onion, adding it to the skewer. "Tell you what. I'll watch the girls tonight if you'll be available Friday evening."

Instantly Flynn thought of Tom Sanders, wondering if she and Tom had a date. "Something special on?"

"Not really, but I'm going out. So, do we have a deal?"

Flynn wasn't sure he was ready to see what was behind door number two, but he nodded. "Sure."

Cindy picked up a chunk of green pepper. "Have fun at the card game."

"Yeah, right." Flynn wasn't able to understand why he suddenly couldn't think of the game, only what Cindy had planned for her night out.

Chapter Eight

†

Cindy rechecked her dangling green rhinestone earrings. They were flashy, but definitely went with the dress. Her makeup, too, was stronger than usual. But on stage, her normal light cosmetics washed out. It was only one of the tricks she'd learned since joining Noah Brady's band.

Despite her lifelong love of music, she'd never considered joining a group. But Noah, once convinced that Cindy had no interest in serious dating, had been relentless, nagging and hounding her until she agreed to participate in a one-time-only gig.

That had been nearly two years ago. Smiling softly, Cindy remembered Noah's disappointment when she'd told him only casual dating was on her agenda. She'd never confided to him about Flynn. No, only Katherine knew of those hopeless feelings. And although she accepted dates, Cindy never encouraged the men to believe she was interested in a serious relationship. If they pressed for anything more, she stopped going out with them.

Noah had been more persistent than any of the others. But also more understanding when he sensed her hidden pain. She hadn't expected to expose that to anyone, and he'd never pressed for details. But she guessed he had figured out it was a hopeless love. So he'd changed tracks, becoming a good and trusted friend. It seemed she'd acquired more big brothers since moving to Rosewood than she could have ever imagined. Michael Carlson, Tom Sanders, Noah Brady. Even though she'd never had a brother, she couldn't imagine a blood relative being any more dependable and concerned for her welfare.

Leaning forward, she inspected her outfit in the cheval mirror that stood in the corner of her room. Tonight's dance was a high school reunion, and the green glitz of her dress would be perfect since it was one of the school's team colors.

Hearing the doorbell ring, she also heard the scrabble of little feet as they trod across the entry hall floor. Although she'd cautioned the girls not to answer the door, they considered it a game, always trying to outrun "Cinny" to welcome whoever stood on the porch.

Luckily it was Noah, who immediately made the girls giggle with delight as he produced three puppets, demonstrating how they worked, then handing them to the girls.

Soon they were settled in the parlor. Noah didn't take one of the chairs or a place on the fainting couch. Instead he chose the piano bench, running his fingers lightly over the keys.

"No late cases?" Cindy asked him, referring to his medical practice.

"Nope. Cleared the calendar." Strong, sculptured fingers that performed with such perfection in the operating room danced over the keys.

Despite their fascination with the puppets he had brought them, the girls were drawn to the music, especially since Noah chose to play a children's song. And within a short time, they were crowded on the bench beside him.

After a few rousing songs, Beth tried to plunk her stubby fingers on the keys. Unruffled, Noah started teaching them the basic notes of "Chopsticks." Delighted, they all reached toward the piano at once. Good with kids, Noah completed the uneven quartet.

Soon, more laughter than music filled the room.

And that was how Flynn found them. He could hear the strains of piano music from the front steps. But it was the laughter that intrigued him. Recognizing his daughters' giggles, his own smile grew.

Until he stepped into the parlor.

Cindy stood directly behind a man Flynn didn't recognize. And his girls were bunched beside him on the bench. It was a cozy picture.

A far-too-cozy picture.

Flynn's jaw tightened. Who was this man now charming both Cindy and his daughters?

Laughter and music continued to fill the old house, drowning out the sounds of his entrance. Although the girls kept their attention on the pianist, Cindy turned suddenly.

It surprised him. Why was she the only one to notice him?

Her hand came down lightly on the man's shoulder and he stopped playing. The girls, finally sensing Flynn's presence, jumped down from the bench, hurtling toward him.

He knelt down, accepting their hugs, gratified by their response.

Then Beth held up a small puppet. "Look what Noah gave me!"

"We played piano, too," Mandy added also holding up her puppet.

Even little Alice displayed hers, a soft bunny-shaped toy.

"Well, isn't that nice," Flynn managed as he stood back up.

The man had risen from the piano bench. He approached, extending his hand. "Noah Brady."

Flynn accepted the handshake, offering his own name. "Looks like you've won over my daughters."

Noah shrugged. "I love kids. Don't have any of my own so it's a pleasure to spend time with someone else's."

"Right," Flynn agreed, wondering who he was. What he meant to Cindy.

Belatedly he realized Noah was dressed in a tux and Cindy was wearing a sparkling deep green gown, one that made her hair look like fire. It was equally clear they were dressed for a very special evening. Ignoring a squiggle of unwanted, insensible resentment, he reached for the anchor of his daughters' hands.

But Beth wriggled away. "Dr. Noah's gonna show us more piano."

Dr. Noah? Flynn glanced pointedly at Cindy.

"Noah's a surgeon," she explained. "Which is probably why he has the right touch for music."

The right touch. Perhaps that wasn't confined only to music. It seemed the man was capable of making Cindy smile and laugh with abandon.

Cindy corralled Beth. "Dr. Noah will have to show you how to play another time. Otherwise we'll be late."

"Me go, too!" Beth demanded.

"Not this time, sweetie," Cindy replied. "This is a grown-ups-only evening."

Flynn wondered why the words felt like ground glass beneath tender, bare feet.

"You come back?" Mandy asked Noah.

"Sure. I love having a captive audience. But Cindy's right. We'd better be going." Again he extended his hand to Flynn. "Good to meet you. Hate to steal Cindy away, but the evening wouldn't be complete without her."

No, Flynn supposed, it wouldn't.

Cindy pulled an exquisitely beaded shawl from the hall rack, then picked up a tiny jeweled bag from the hall table. "We shouldn't be too late."

Flynn stared at her, wondering who this dazzlingly beautiful woman was. Normally dressed in jeans or overalls, she now looked like an exotic stranger. One who was going out with the handsome doctor. Struggling to maintain his composure, Flynn nodded.

"Fine. The girls and I will probably order a pizza."

"Whatever you think," she replied easily.

Where was her normal lecture on the benefits of healthy eating? Had the good doctor turned Cindy's head so much she didn't give the girls' welfare a passing thought?

But before the notion could process, Noah swept Cindy outside, the duo looking perfectly suited. Flynn bit down on the thought, but it escaped nonetheless.

He should be glad, happy Cindy had found such a person. Instead, all he could feel was a growing wall of resentment.

Cicadas and bullfrogs filled the night air with their own sort of music, accentuating the solitary hoot of a secluded owl.

The lonely sound fitted Flynn's mood. Any other time he would appreciate the scent of the native honeysuckle that roamed through the trees and over the weathered fence. But he'd been restless most of the evening. That had only increased since he'd put the girls to bed. Because then his mind could wander without distraction.

Flynn took a deep breath, inhaling clean air that wasn't tinged with big-city smog.

Flynn wondered if Cindy and Noah were dancing beneath the stars that stood out so clearly in the uncluttered sky. No reflection from thousands of lights dimmed the deep midnight color. Everything about this place was so different than what he was used to.

And he didn't want to dwell on the fact that Cindy was the most different of all.

He stood that way for a long time, hearing the quiet neighborhood sounds, ones that were now familiar to him. Mr. Elliott next door put out his cat. Mrs. Anderson whose backyard aligned with Cindy's, called for her little poodle, then closed and locked her door once he was inside. And somewhere not too far away, he could the distant strains of a teenager's music.

The theme for the evening — music.

The thought barely surfaced when he caught the drifting scent of a new fragrance. Recognizing it, he spun around, not willing to be part of a possible good-night kiss between Cindy and her date.

But she stood alone, framed by the ancient French doors, before cautiously stepping out on the terrace. "Flynn? Is that you?"

"Yes. Didn't mean to get in your way."

She stepped closer. "I'm not sure what you mean."

"Isn't Noah with you?"

She shook her head. "Well . . . no. Are the girls asleep?"

"Hours ago. Although I still can't get them settled in as quickly as you do."

She shrugged a slim shoulder, partially exposed by the narrow straps of her dress. "It's not a contest."

"So it isn't."

Silence slithered between them, broken only by another call of the distant owl.

Cindy stepped out of her strappy high-heeled sandals, her voice as soft as her face. "My feet are killing me."

A night of dancing would do that. "I imagine so."

"It's pretty out here at night, isn't it?" she mused, her face dreamy beneath the partial moonlight.

Flynn wondered if Noah had put that expression on her face.

"I'm usually so caught up in one thing or another that I don't appreciate what's literally in my own backyard," she continued.

Mr. Elliott opened a side door and coaxed in his cat. One final meow was cut off by the closing door.

"So, does this Noah guy go to your church, too?" Flynn asked, hoping he sounded appropriately casual.

She paused for a moment, crickets filling in the silence. "Yes, that's where we met. He's the musical director."

Flynn frowned into the darkness. "I thought he was a doctor."

"He is. A plastic surgeon. But he volunteers as the musical director for our church. We don't have a large budget — certainly not one that would stretch to include a paid musical director. We had a fire a few years ago that we're still paying for. Besides, Noah's incredibly talented. He once considered music instead of medicine."

"And which profession suffered the most from his choice?"

She laughed, a quiet, skeptical sound. "Neither. He gives his all to his patients when he's at the hospital. And he absolutely inspires the kids and teenagers at church. He's helped to turn around more than one wayward child by including them in the choir."

"Practically a saint," Flynn muttered.

"What?"

"The girls were very impressed by him. They want you to invite him over again."

She shrugged. "No problem. I see Noah often. And if he's coming to pick me up, and his schedule permits, he can arrive a little early, see the girls."

Flynn stiffened, glad that the blackness of the night hid the motion. "I'm sure they'd like that."

155

Another silence vibrated between them. But the crickets weren't enough to fill the gap this time.

"Is something wrong, Flynn?"

He shook his head. "Nah. There's something about the quiet that makes a person think, evaluate."

"Funny, we fill up nearly every moment with television, music, computers or conversation. One of the downfalls of modern technology, I suppose."

But Flynn wasn't in the mood for small talk. "Why didn't you invite Noah to the party you gave to introduce me to your friends?"

"I did. He had an emergency call and didn't leave the hospital all night. It's hard for him to know if he'll ever be able to keep plans he's made."

"That must be annoying," Flynn remarked.

She shrugged. "He doesn't really seem to mind. He's so dedicated. And he just shuffles other commitments. He has a lot of friends who step in when there's a real crunch."

"He sounds almost too good to be true."

She laughed again. "I thought the same thing when I met him. But now I know him well enough to realize he's the genuine article."

So Cindy was infatuated with the town hero. That should be a comfort. He wondered why it wasn't.

He glanced over at her, realizing she was only a handspan away. Again the subtle scent of her perfume snagged his attention. He had only to reach out and he could touch her, catch her hand within his.

She turned, meeting his gaze. "I'm glad we've been able to work things out, that we can trade off watching the girls as we need to. I want you to feel that Rosewood is really becoming your home, that you can find wonderful friends here, as well."

"Friends like Noah?" he questioned, watching her face.

But her pretty features didn't give anything away. "Exactly. You couldn't ask for better people than Noah or Michael or Tom."

It was an innocent statement, absolutely guileless, equally unrevealing.

She hitched up the shawl, covering her arms. "I'd better head inside. As much as I enjoy the night sky, the girls will be up early." She smiled. "And I need my beauty sleep."

He watched as she walked away and into the house. That's where she was wrong. With or without sleep, Cindy was a beauty.

And it seemed the men in this small town weren't blind to the fact. Staring again into the ever-deepening darkness, he wondered why that, too, was a thought he couldn't shake.

Chapter Nine

†

Cindy finished snapping the last overall strap in place. She grinned, just looking at the triplets, thinking surely they were the most lovable children on earth.

Alice, the child who clung the closest and had bonded inseparably with her, reached for her hand.

"You all look great," Cindy complimented them, glad she'd picked different color T-shirts for each one. Purple, kelly green and bright yellow.

All of the clothes Flynn had brought with him were things Cindy considered more appropriate for dress-up occasions.

"Daddy!" Beth hollered, seeing Flynn in the hall.

He turned into the room with a smile that faded faster than ice cream on a hot summer sidewalk.

"Me pretty?" Mandy asked again, this time directing the question to Flynn.

Seeing the displeasure on his face, Cindy motioned with a shake of her head for him not to say what was obviously on his mind.

"I'm sure Daddy always thinks you're pretty."

"Sure, punkin," Flynn replied. "Why don't you and your sisters head downstairs? You can get the granola out. But no running."

They took off with typical toddler speed, but the sound of their sneakers slowed down as they reached the stairs, having been properly impressed by the danger of falling down the wide, wooden steps.

"What's with the overalls?" Flynn asked as soon as they heard the girls successfully navigate the stairs.

Taken aback, Cindy stared at him. "I'm not sure what you mean."

"I don't consider overalls proper attire for my daughters."

Cindy hesitated, remembering all too well the frilly dresses Julia always put them in. "How do you expect them to run and play if they're dressed like porcelain dolls?"

He waved away the concern. "It's never been a problem."

Cindy wouldn't criticize her late sister if it meant biting her tongue until it sliced clear through. Yet, she couldn't relent on this point. "They're not fragile dolls meant to be put on a shelf. They're real children who need to run and get dirty, and maybe scrape a knee." A new thought prodded her. "Is that what you're worried about? That they'll get hurt if they play like other children?"

His mouth tightened and Cindy wondered what past demon still possessed him.

"I'm not blasé about my children's safety. And I don't understand your attitude. Why are you so willing to assume they'll be all right?"

Cindy blinked, nearly taking a step backward from the wrath she saw in his eyes. "Flynn, I care terribly about their welfare. I, too, have lost everyone in my family. I don't want to lose anyone else. Especially the girls. But you can't lock them away, either." Taking a chance, she continued. "I know that's what Julia tried to do. She never got over the fact that if Dad hadn't insisted on so much adventure, he and Mom would be alive. But they had to live as they did, including that last boat ride. There was something in Dad that pushed him to carve every bit out of every minute. And Mom loved him enough to understand that. It was an accident, a dreadful, sad, unfortunate accident, but it wasn't some sort of morbid legacy. I'm sorry if Julia brought that worry to your marriage and transferred it to the girls. But keeping them from life won't keep them alive."

His jaw tightened even further. "Don't meddle in things you know nothing about."

"Nothing? They were my parents, too, and —"

"But the triplets are *my* children, not yours. I'll decide what's best for them."

Cindy pushed past the pain of his reminder, one that said no matter how she'd grown to love the girls, they would never be hers. "Of course they're *your* daughters. But I do care desperately about them, as well. And I certainly don't think wearing overalls and T-shirts will scar them for life."

He snorted impatiently. "What's next? Jeans and cigars?"

She smiled, despite the unresolved tension. "Jeans maybe. But I'll hold off on the cigars."

Flynn's glance lifted to encompass the picture of Jesus that still hung on the wall. The unspoken reminder of his displeasure lingered between them.

He pivoted toward the door.

But Cindy reached out, catching his arm.

The contact seared between them.

As quickly she dropped her own hand. "I — I was wondering if you'd like to go with us to the park. I promised the girls. We could make a morning of it, take some lunch along."

Flynn's eyes remained dark, unrevealing. "I have to go into the office. I'm interviewing some applicants today."

She nodded. "I see."

His gaze searched hers again. However, just when Cindy thought he was about to say something, he turned, leaving the room.

And again she wondered.

The park was perfect. Spring in the Texas Hill Country meant mild temperatures, often sunny skies. And wildflowers colored all the fields beyond the manicured lawns of the park.

The girls spotted the seesaw and squealed as they headed straight for it. Cindy didn't mind. She knew they would all try to get on one side and they'd be safe until she put the cooler on a redwood table beneath the shaded canopy of tall oak trees.

Beth, Mandy and Alice all sat on one side as she'd predicted. Plucking Mandy from the trio, she put her on the other end, using her own weight to help Mandy move up and down. When they finally tired of the seesaw, they were off to the swings, then the slide, the sandbox and the monkey bars. By then they were ready for the seesaw again.

She put Mandy and Beth on one end this

time and took her place with Alice, reaching out to pull the child down so Mandy and Beth could rise.

"Any room on there for me?" Flynn asked from beside her.

Startled, she let the board go, snapping Alice back into place. "Sorry, sweetie."

"Tell you what," Flynn offered. "I'll sit with Alice and you sit with Mandy and Beth."

He looked as though he expected her to refuse. But she'd seldom met a challenge she'd capitulated to. So she walked to the other end, pulling the girls down and sitting behind them.

Flynn easily pulled down all their weight with one arm and climbed on the seesaw behind Alice.

Cindy tried to be cautious, but Flynn's strong legs pumped them quickly up and down. Within a few minutes, she was laughing along with the girls, their giggles and hoots filling the quiet playground.

Nearly winded, Cindy was ready to call for a time-out. But a new, unexpected twinkle flashed in Flynn's eyes. And she couldn't resist the dare lurking in them.

It felt as though they were almost flying as the seesaw moved up and down, again and again. Even so, they were careful to keep a secure grip on the girls. It was Flynn who finally slowed the pace when the girls began to tire.

"No, Daddy!" they chorused.

But Flynn plucked them off one by one.

"Okay, girls. Let's head to the table. Time for some lunch."

"And a nap," Cindy said quietly, reaching down to pick a wildflower, knowing the girls would be so exhausted they'd probably fall asleep in the car on the way home.

Although they protested, each one came to the table. "I thought you had to be at the office," Cindy commented, pulling at the stem of the buttercup.

"The interviews didn't take long."

Cindy wondered if he'd rushed the interviews so he could join them. As quickly she dismissed the notion.

"Did you find anyone you liked?"

"Actually, all three that showed up."

"Is it going to be hard to choose?" she asked.

"No. I hired all of them."

Surprised, Cindy glanced up at him. "Do you have that much work for them to do?"

"If my concept's valid."

Concern mixed with her other feelings. "Do they know it's a risk?"

"Sure. I wouldn't let someone assume a

sense of security that's not certain. But they seemed to think it was a risk worth taking."

Cindy nodded. "I only asked because new jobs aren't that plentiful in Rosewood. Even Adair Petroleum brought in their own people for the new regional office. I'd hate to see someone give up a secure job and then wind up unemployed."

"I may not be a member of your religious circle, but I don't cheat or lie, either."

She bit back at the exasperation bubbling to be heard. "Of course you don't. And belonging to a church isn't about judging others. In fact, it's just the opposite."

"Not in my experience."

"What is that experience, Flynn?" she asked quietly.

"Doesn't do any good to dwell on the past. It's gone, unchangeable."

She searched his eyes, seeing a wealth of pain he usually concealed well. "If it would help you to deal with today —"

"I have to depend on myself, Cindy. Myself alone. I learned that a long time ago. And talk of church won't change that."

"It's not just talk, not to me, despite what you believe."

"Has your faith brought back your mother, your father . . . Julia?" Bleakness so cold, it stole away the warmth of the day, surfaced in his eyes. "I didn't think so."

"But —"

"And you'll move past this phase too, Cindy. You think I'm saying this to be cruel, but that's not it. You shouldn't be sucked in by a myth any more than I should. Myths don't protect and nurture."

Feeling the pain of his tortured soul in her own, she reached for his hand. "Despite what you think of me, my scattered ways, the way I poorly compare to Julia, don't let that stand between you and the truth."

He glanced down at their clasped hands.

Feeling the heat of his gaze, she slowly withdrew her own.

"The truth is I haven't believed God existed since I was nine years old. Meeting all your church friends, even liking them or considering them my new friends, allowing the girls to attend Sunday school, playing on the church softball team, none of that will change how I believe." He glanced at the table where the girls were happily digging into the chips and cookies. "You live a fairy tale, Cindy, and I don't want to take that away from you. But don't think you'll change me. Ever. Because it won't happen."

Cindy forced her stiff legs forward, her body numb from his words. Was that truly how he felt? Would he never, never change his views about his faith? And if not, where did that leave her love for him?

Closing her eyes, she remembered the past painful years, ones spent silently loving him. Reality struck like a slap across the face. Even if he could eventually come to love her, she couldn't spend her life with a man of no faith.

And she'd thought convincing him that she'd changed was her largest obstacle. Now, it seemed a minor bump in the road in comparison. Yet, it, too, was a mammoth barrier. For the first time since she'd met Flynn Mallory, Cindy faced the truth. They weren't meant to be together, not then, not now. Never.

Even though Flynn had no use for religious holidays, he tolerated those with secular meaning, as well. So he had expected Cindy to color Easter eggs and fill baskets for the girls.

But returning home from the office, he was stunned to see Cindy's charity kids all grouped around the kitchen table, as well. A dozen bowls held all shades of dye and it looked as though Cindy had boiled at least six dozen eggs for decoration.

Cindy, like the kids, seemed to be wearing an undue amount of dye, as well.

168

"Any dye left for the eggs?" he asked, coming closer to the table.

Cindy glanced up at him, then down at her messy hands and arms. "Possibly a drop or two." Quickly she introduced the children. Flynn smiled at them in turn.

The triplets, imitating Cindy, held out their arms, as well. Alongside the light-tinted dye stains were deep streaks of color.

Flynn's tolerant smile faded. "Are you sure that washes off?"

Cindy followed his gaze. Her patient smile dimmed. "That doesn't look like the egg dye."

Ricky held up a black marker. "We found these in the crayon drawer."

Cindy's eyes widened. Reaching out, she took the marker from him, then collected the others. "These are permanent markers, Ricky. We don't use these to color on anything. They're mine for making signs. Are you sure they were in the crayon drawer?"

Six-year-old Ricky shrugged. "I dunno. Paul and me found 'em."

Cindy glanced up at Flynn. "Sorry. I didn't realize they'd gotten into these."

"So they're not going to wash off?"

She shook her head. "Not for a while anyway."

"Great. They'll look as though they've been tattooed."

Cindy looked first at the triplets, then back at Flynn, inserting a placating note in her voice. "They can wear long sleeves till it fades."

Flynn rolled his eyes. "And you plan to take them to church tomorrow looking like that?"

Cindy's smile wavered. "I'll find something for them to wear."

He glanced around the messy, cluttered kitchen, but didn't say anything. What was the point? As though she could pull together this fiasco, clean up the children *and* find them something to wear for the next day. It was of no concern to him. Flynn didn't want the girls to attend anyway. At first he'd considered Sunday school simply a social thing, but he didn't want the girls to make connections that would be difficult to break.

And he was certain Cindy wasn't committed enough to the church to spend the night assembling outfits for the triplets.

Easter morning dawned, bright and beautiful. So much so, that it seemed perfect, Cindy realized, as she hemmed the last small dress.

Flynn had been right. She had scrubbed the girls' arms as vigorously as possible during bath time, yet the stains wouldn't budge. And nothing the girls owned would completely cover the permanent ink marks on their arms. A quick trip to the children's store had been fruitless, as well. Being spring, all the dresses had short sleeves.

But Cindy wasn't ready to admit defeat. Returning home, she'd searched her project closet, unearthing a bolt of white material that had been intended for church tablecloths. Since she'd purchased pink hats and socks to go with their short-sleeved Easter dresses, Cindy was certain she could come up with something appropriate.

Using an older dress for a pattern, Cindy cut out three little dresses. Once sewn, the dresses still lacked something. Rooting through her project materials, Cindy almost squealed when she unearthed two full rolls of wide pink ribbon. She had once used a third roll to make congratulatory ribbons for the kids. Now she was certain it would make the perfect accent for the pristine white dresses. It didn't take long to braid the pink ribbon with a bit of lace, forming sashes.

Although Cindy was tired by morning, she was also pleased. Making dresses for the girls was far more satisfying than purchasing them. And now she decided the pure white dresses with their simple sash belts were far prettier than the short-sleeved floral ones she'd purchased.

Skipping downstairs to grab a cup of coffee, she was surprised to see Flynn in the kitchen. "It's early for you, isn't it?"

"I know you're disappointed that the girls won't be able to go to church, so I'm making breakfast."

" 'O, ye of little faith.' "

He frowned. "We're not going into that again, are we? I've allowed the girls to go to Sunday school because it seems mostly playing and coloring and singing at their age. But —"

She held up one hand. "I'm a little tired for a theological debate this morning. Besides, it's Easter. Let's not spoil that."

He handed her a mug of coffee. "Why are you so tired?"

She smiled. "I've been up sewing."

"*You* know how to sew?"

"You really do think Julia and I were conceived on different planets." She waved away his attempt to explain or apologize. It really didn't matter which. "Yes, I know how to sew. I made the girls new dresses for today — long-sleeved dresses." She took a healthy sip of coffee, then glanced at him. "You can close your mouth now."

"Sorry. But what possessed you to do that?"

Meeting his questioning gaze, all she could feel was sadness so immense, it wearied her far more than the sleepless night. "I don't think you can possibly understand." She gripped her mug closer. "And that makes me the one who's sorry."

Turning away before she could see his stunned face, Cindy jogged up the stairs, escaping the questions, but embracing the day. She took comfort in the beautiful Easter morning, knowing the agony it cost Flynn to stand alone. Also knowing she was powerless to change his unyielding views. But it was Easter, the day of new promises and life. And time to put this dilemma in His hands.

Chapter Ten

†

The next few weeks were tense. Flynn hadn't wanted to unleash more of his past. But all of Cindy's questions did just that.

Funny though, escaping from Cindy had pushed him into a closer friendship with Michael Carlson and Tom Sanders. He still felt the instant kinship he'd shared with Michael since the first time they'd met. He'd been far more reluctant to accept Tom as a friend, remembering too well how chummy the other man seemed to be with Cindy. He refused to put a name to why that bothered him, but it hadn't made him want Tom as a friend.

Then, during one of their card games, Flynn had learned inadvertently that Tom Sanders wasn't a romantic interest. Tom referred to her as the little sister he'd never had, but one he was glad to have in his life. The words were genuine and true, Flynn realized with a touch of shame.

But that didn't relieve Flynn's thoughts fully. There was still Noah Brady to consider. And the good doctor didn't come to their friendly card games; his crowded schedule too full.

It didn't matter, Flynn told himself. Cindy could date whomever she wanted. That nagging feeling in his gut was no doubt a brotherly concern of his own. An inner voice told him that reasoning didn't ring true, but he ignored it. And each day, like today, it had been on his mind as he worked.

The house was quiet as he entered. It had been a long day at the office — too long. Quietly walking upstairs, he was disappointed to find that the girls were already asleep. It was his own fault, Flynn realized. The same mistake he'd made when Julia had been alive. Resolving not to let it happen again, Flynn passed Cindy's room, seeing that it was empty. He searched the rest of the house, looking for her.

She was out on the terrace. Sitting in one of her aged, fan-shaped wicker chairs, Cindy had a tall glass of what looked to be lemonade on the round wrought-iron table. A pitcher and a second empty glass sat on one of her painted, wooden trays. The arbor shaded the last of the sun's evening rays, creating a dappled illusion of shape and shadow.

Cindy could have stepped out from the confines of a Renoir canvas, Flynn realized suddenly. Her vibrant hair and eyes, the old-fashioned sundress, her clear porcelain skin.

He could tell she didn't hear him approaching, his soft-leather-soled shoes making little noise on the faded red cobbled stones.

Cindy was intently studying a tall, wide book. Without the unceasing tension that normally separated them, she looked gentler . . . soft even. Nothing about Cindy ever said soft.

Wild, impulsive, adventurous. But never soft.

Still he gentled his own tone, trying to quiet the intrusion. "Hey."

She didn't jump, instead finally looking up at him as though reluctantly pulled from another world. Cindy belonged to another world, he realized suddenly. She could have fit in as easily in Victorian days as she did in the present. Her vivaciousness and quick wit would have made her a darling of society.

As he watched, her lips turned upward gently, not her usual wide grin, rather a soft sloping that revealed tenderness rather than mirth. "Hey, yourself."

He gestured to one of the other chairs loosely gathered around the table. "Do

176

you mind if I join you?"

She shook her head. "I thought you might be coming home soon. The other glass is for you. I made limeade."

Of course. No traditional lemonade for nontraditional Cindy.

As he sat, she tipped the pitcher, filling his glass.

Now wanting to disturb the unusual, peaceful moment, he sipped the brew, finding it surprisingly good.

"It's the maraschino cherries," she told him before he could ask. "Sweetens without being too sweet."

Again he nodded, enjoying the tranquil moment. Relaxing in the oversize chair, he wondered at this woman of many moods. "What are you reading?"

"A party planner. It has all kinds of great ideas for kids parties."

Surprised, he hadn't expected her to need a guide. Her life used to be one endless party. Of course, that was before he'd burst on to the scene, bringing his three children and a weight of responsibility. "You thinking about a party?"

She smiled at him ruefully. "Oh, Flynn."

Calmed by the surroundings, even her tone could scarcely stir him. "Yes?"

"The girls' birthday. Next week. I want it

to be extraspecial. The last one . . . well . . . you know."

The last one had been too soon after Julia's passing for him to celebrate it properly. Uncomfortably Flynn remembered that he hadn't invited Cindy to the last-minute, toned-down birthday dinner. Only Flynn and the girls had been there. He had been ill at ease in the kiddy pizza place, the girls unhappy without their mother or Aunt Cindy.

And now it was time to plan another celebration. "Funny. I thought about it for months afterward, how I would make it up to them, taking the time to arrange something really special for the next birthday."

"Perhaps you put it out of your mind because it reminded you of more difficult times."

"Regret." The word was surprisingly bitter in the calm of the night. "I've had my fill of it."

Cindy's gaze softened further. "Flynn, you can't blame yourself for things no one can control."

"Who do I blame?" he asked with less rancor, trying to match his tone to the mood of the night. "Your God?"

Agony darkened her bright green eyes and impulsively she laid one hand over his. "Is that what you want your daughters to believe?"

"I want them to understand you have to be strong on your own, that you can't depend on anyone or anything in this life other than yourself."

Cindy swallowed, her expression so earnest, it was nearly painful. "What about friends, the people who care about you? Ones who like you for who you are, not who you want to be? Who accept you, flaws and all, maybe liking you even more for having them. Do you want to shut them out of your life, too?"

Flynn considered her words, the depth of her sincerity. Depth? From Cindy? The girl he'd met that long-ago night hadn't possessed depth. What she had possessed was like the lure of molten gold. Beautiful, but capable of burning when touched.

"What about you, Cindy? I've listened, observed. But you've never told me. Why did you come to Rosewood? What made you hide yourself so far away from your own friends and only family? You told me that you knew just Katherine when you moved here. Even Julia didn't know about your plans until a few days before you left. What's the big secret, Cindy? Why did *you* run away?"

Her mouth opened, but no words emerged. Instead she handed him the book she'd been reading. Then thrusting back her chair, she fled. Spry and slim, she disappeared into the house.

Left with only the night sounds for company, Flynn dropped his forehead against one splayed hand. What had come over him? Because she had pushed him, he knew, looking for answers. And he couldn't bear to repeat the painful memories. So he'd pushed back, taking the offense instead of the defense.

Lifting his head, he glanced at the book she'd shoved into his hands. A piece of paper marked her place. On it she'd drawn a spectacular rendering of a child's birthday party. One that seemed nearly as magical as the dreams all little girls should have.

And then he wondered what had happened to Cindy's dreams. A passionate person, she must have once held lustrous hopes. And no matter what she said, he doubted those had begun or ended in Rosewood.

Paper lanterns fluttered gently in the breeze, lending an old-fashioned aura to the festive backyard. But they fit well with the antique wicker chairs and long, curving wrought-iron benches. The lattice arbor continued to shade the terrace where Cindy had set up several round tables. Each was covered by a rose- or daisy-patterned tablecloth that trailed to the ground. And she'd scattered just enough iridescent glitter over them that they sparkled in the sun. The largest table was already stacked with presents.

Knowing the kids wouldn't want to remain seated at a long table, she had instead put punch and cups on one table, small plates with nuts and candy on another.

Although three sparkly tables were set aside for each of the girls' birthday cakes, the actual desserts remained inside under wraps. She had chosen three separate shapes, flavors and colors to give each girl a special, individual birthday experience.

"It's coming together," Flynn commented, tacking up a Pin-the-Tail-on-the-Donkey game.

Cindy nodded. "We've planned enough games to keep them occupied, and then of course, there's the pony you rented."

He winced. "Okay, maybe *I* am the one spoiling them. But the pony will only be here for a few hours. It's not like I got them a stable."

She placed a stack of games on a side table. "Only because there's not enough room in my backyard, and your new yard's still being torn up by bulldozers."

"I wasn't planning on a stable for nearly another year or two," he retorted, a smile twitching on his lips.

She grinned, as well.

He glanced at the swing set that she had covered in streamers and balloons, then to the edge of the decorated arbor. She had wound streamers decorated with unicorns and delicate ballerinas among them all.

His gaze traveled to the dozen child-pro-portioned chairs and tables, which had been set with plates, cups and plastic forks, scattered throughout the yard. The multiple colors of the tablecloths resembled those of a box of spilled crayons. "And you didn't go a little overboard yourself?"

She shrugged. "You know me. I go overboard with everything."

For a moment he didn't reply, the tension that never left them, surging again.

"Besides, I borrowed the kiddie furniture from the church."

He lifted his brow.

"Katherine said it was okay. And you can help me haul it back."

"After scraping up sticky plates and cups,

that should be a treat," Flynn replied easily. Then he spotted Noah Brady entering the yard through the side gate, as though he'd done it every day of his life. The man seemed uncommonly comfortable in Cindy's home.

She turned to follow his gaze. "Oh, good! Noah's here with his electronic keyboard. I thought the kids would like the music."

"You haven't heard of a CD player?" Flynn retorted.

She drew her brows together. "Live music's a little more fun. Besides, I've drafted a few other players. The kids will love it."

Flynn forced his thoughts to settle. This was his daughters' birthday party, not the time to question Cindy's personal life. Still, he watched as she rushed over to Noah, her smile wide and open. It occurred to him that the only time he saw that same smile on her face was when she was with someone other than him. As Flynn had suspected, Noah knew how to make her smile. . . . Evidently he was a man who came with no irksome baggage that precluded easy smiles.

Katherine and Michael Carlson, along with their children, arrived next. David, Annie and Danny immediately joined the triplets.

Flynn watched the Carlson family, still

amazed that the couple had been together for such a short time. Not only did they seem ideally suited, but Katherine was openly loving and tender with all three children. Flynn was certain that no one would take them for a blended family. But then he guessed their relationship was an exception.

Michael raised a hand in greeting. Although Flynn was accustomed to keeping people at a distance, Michael was one of the few people Flynn had met who were simply and exactly what they seemed. No pretense, no agendas. Through softball and card games, he'd come to consider Michael a friend.

Michael crossed the yard. "Katherine and Cindy have their heads together, and I'm guessing we're about to be drafted soon."

Flynn found himself grinning. "That sounds like it was said from experience."

"You wouldn't believe what those two can dream up. You should have seen Annie's first birthday party after we married. You'd have thought our house and yard had been taken over by a Barbie army. I saw pink for days."

Flynn chuckled. "Barbie army, huh?"

"Don't laugh. Wait'll your girls are a little older. We've had tea parties that would send a sane man running for his life. You haven't lived till you've come home to a dozen little girls dressed in hats and high heels and your wife acting as though it's the most natural thing on earth."

Flynn winced in male sympathy. "But you do have sons, as well."

"Don't even get me started on that. For David's party, she had everyone dress like cowboys and cowgirls and she rented not one, not two, but three ponies. My yard looked like I'd been housing a herd of wild mustangs."

Flynn tried not to laugh. "So, you're telling me Katherine has a lot of . . . um . . . creativity."

"More than enough. But it's not just her. She and Cindy came up with both plans. Alone they're fascinating. Together they're positively explosive. You sure the circus isn't planning to appear in the backyard today?"

"Nah. I wanted a pony. Cindy wanted a clown, but we agreed the pony alone would be best."

Michael glanced around the yard. "You seen Cindy since we got here?"

Flynn shook his head.

Michael's brows rose. "I was wondering why Katherine brought along an overnight bag. Ten to one, either she or Cindy makes an appearance dressed as a clown."

"But she wouldn't —"

Michael's chuckle cut off his words. "Oh, Flynn, my man. You don't know these women very well yet."

"I don't think Cindy would really do that."

Michael's hearty laugh echoed in the quiet yard. "Are you kidding? The two of them might burst through a flaming hoop!" He clapped a hand on Flynn's shoulder. "Buck up. You just have to realize that Cindy's got an endless imagination."

"A corked barrel of dynamite," Flynn replied.

"I'm wrong. You do know her."

"I did once," Flynn admitted. "I'm not quite so sure now."

Some of the male camaraderie faded from Michael's expression. "I consider Cindy's passionate spirit her best quality. It makes her who she is."

And that was the problem. Yet Flynn only nodded.

Michael, in tune with Flynn's change in mood, glanced toward the yard. "So what can I do to help?"

"Cindy's got most of it set up. She's been up since dawn."

Michael chuckled. "When she was

186

working on the church after the fire, we had to pry her down from the scaffolding. You'd have thought she had experience working on skyscrapers the way she climbed up and around that stuff."

"She mentioned the fire briefly. What happened?"

"Old wiring. It leveled the sanctuary. But with a legion of volunteers like Cindy, we were able to salvage most of the original stone and brick. That's why the building doesn't look squeaky new."

Flynn lifted a brow skeptically. "You mean Cindy was doing the work herself instead of writing a check?"

Michael's face reflected his own surprise. "Why would you think she'd do that?"

Flynn shrugged. "The Cindy I've known never lasted very long with these fads of hers. Julia told me Cindy tried a half-dozen different occupations since we married, never staying with one long enough to see if it suited her. I honestly don't believe this is any more than another craze."

"Then maybe you don't know Cindy as well as you think," Michael replied quietly. "And that's a shame."

Flynn glanced over at Noah, who was running an extension cord for the keyboard and speakers. "I think there are plenty of other people in Cindy's life who know her well."

Michael kept his own counsel. "Maybe so."

Flynn wasn't sure why, but he sensed disappointment from Michael. Since they were still only new friends, Flynn wasn't certain why this bothered him.

So he directed his gaze back to Noah. However, as he watched, a stream of children entered from the side gate. Cindy's Rainbow kids. And it looked like both sets, from her two classes. Perfect.

"Cindy's worked miracles with these kids," Michael said, following his gaze.

Flynn continued watching them. "Yeah. Cookies and Play-Doh will do that."

Michael shook his head. "You don't have a clue, do you?"

"I don't mean to be rude, but this isn't going to be a religious lecture, is it?"

"That, too?" Michael asked in a knowing tone. "I should have guessed. But maybe it's true, sharing a problem doesn't make you recognize it in someone else. Like ex-alcoholics, smokers . . . and disbelievers. You'd think there'd be some sign of unity, but I guess we hide it because we don't want to think about it, examine it too closely."

"I don't know what you're talking about."

"Until I met Katherine I was in the same place you are. Happy as I am now, it's hard to think about that time. But if you need someone who understands, someone who was there, when you're ready I'll be around."

The kids started hollering, clapping madly.

Flynn and Michael glanced in their direction, seeing Katherine stepping through the French doors with a clown.

"It was an even call," Michael told him with a rueful note of glee. "But yours is the clown this time."

Yours. Did Michael really see Cindy that way? As the woman in his life?

Watching her, Flynn couldn't imagine two such ill-suited people.

Cindy had swept her luxurious, flaming hair into a multitude of ponytails. And her face was covered in white grease paint, her eyes, nose and lips blatantly outlined. Two bright spots of red circled her cheeks and she was dressed in orange and purple polka dots and a lime-green checkered plaid. It looked as though she'd wound at least a dozen scarves around her neck and waist. Her hands were covered by oversize cotton garden gloves in a wild floral print. She looked outrageous, unlikely and entirely unique. Much like her personality.

The older kids tugged her toward the backyard while the triplets stared at her with a sort of confused fascination and then started running toward her, as well.

When they reached her, Cindy made each of the triplets stand alone for a moment as she individually introduced them to the other children's cheers.

"Are you going to do magic tricks?" young Ricky asked.

She frowned, walking over to him and bending down slightly. Her hands rested first on his shoulders, then one moved over his ear, producing a quarter. "I'm not sure you can afford my magic tricks," she teased him, plopping the quarter into his hands.

As Flynn watched, Cindy performed a few simple tricks. But the children, unsophisticated and eager, clapped for each one.

Then she and Katherine brought out trays of paints and brushes. Face painting, Flynn realized. The children lined up in front of both Cindy and Katherine, eager to have designs painted on their small faces.

Flynn started to turn away when he saw Cindy beckon to him. Thinking she needed more supplies, he knelt beside her, just close enough to speak lowly into her ear, "I thought we'd decided not to have a clown."

Her black outlined brows rose. "Oh, no. That was you." Then she batted her huge false eyelashes. "Besides, I'm a woman of many talents."

Standing up, he smiled at the next child in line, and started to move away.

Cindy snagged his hand, however. "Not so fast. I need another helper."

He stared at her in disbelief. "I don't know how to do this painting thing."

"You can show him," Annie Carlson suggested helpfully.

"Yes, Daddy paint!" Beth cried out.

"Yes!" Mandy and Alice echoed.

Flynn groaned aloud.

But Cindy was already swiveling toward him. "I think you'll need to sit down so I can reach your face."

"You're going to show me on my own face?"

"What better way?" she asked. She motioned with her eyes to the triplets. "You wouldn't want to disappoint them, would you?" It was only because of his daughters that he complied.

"I should have made my escape when I could," Flynn muttered.

Cindy was already dipping her brush into vivid green paint. "Perhaps a butterfly," she mused. "Or a sweet little pink heart."

He looked at the green paint. "The only reason I'm still sitting here is because that paint isn't pink."

She smiled, her perfect white teeth emphasized by the outlandish clown face makeup. "I think you can brave it through pink or green." She lifted the green-coated brush. "But I won't push my luck." Leaning forward, she touched the tip of the feather-light brush against his cheek.

Flynn hadn't known what to expect, a cold slimy glob of paint heated only by his embarrassment perhaps. Instead, her touch was incredibly gentle, much like a warm whisper against his skin.

Angling closer to paint the intricate design, she was mere inches from his face. He could smell the sweet rush of her breath, feel the warmth of her touch. Mesmerized, he sat as though paralyzed, his mind and body captive to her spell.

She had brought a small tray of paints with her and she tilted her face to study them, her forehead only a lock of hair away from his. Reaching up to add some final spots of brown, she paused.

Despite the camouflage of her clown makeup, he could discern the green of her eyes, the wisp of pink as her lips parted. And there was something in her face, something he'd never seen before — the true Cindy. Despite the ludicrous grease paint, her naked emotions were laid bare.

Cindy, all fun and fire. And something within stirred in response.

"Frog on Daddy!" Mandy exclaimed.

He tore his gaze from Cindy's. "What?"

"Frog on you," Mandy explained.

Flynn glanced up at Cindy.

She shrugged a bit sheepishly. "I thought the idea of face painting might make you feel like croaking."

The laugh burst out before Flynn could stop it.

Alice tugged at his sleeve. "Daddy funny?"

"Yes," he managed. "I imagine Daddy looks very funny."

The moment broken, he accepted a tray of paints and a brush. "Me first?" Alice asked.

Flynn glanced at Cindy. "I can't paint as well as she can."

Cindy winked at this shiest triplet. "But Daddy paints with love, and that's lots better than anything else."

"Better," Alice agreed.

And one of the cold places deep inside Flynn thawed a fraction. He had about decided that Alice preferred Cindy hands-down to her own father. Now she wrapped chubby arms around his neck. "Love you."

Hastened by a furnace of emotion, the thawing continued. "I love you, too, punkin."

"Make me a clown like Cinny?" Alice asked, with her sweet smile.

Two worlds, Flynn realized. One they shared with him, one with Cindy.

Flynn did his best, turning often to study Cindy's face, presumably to copy her makeup. But he found his gaze lingering a little too long, a little too often.

When the face painting concluded, they rushed to other games. Even with a piñata dangling temptingly as the final prize, the kids still lingered over the other games.

Flynn, along with the other adults, spread out across the yard. So he was surprised to find himself playing Twister with Cindy.

"I could move on to another game," he offered.

She shrugged. It was neither invitation nor rebuff. Yet he stayed.

It didn't take long for Flynn, Cindy, Annie and David to become snarled in the game. The kids giggled as first Flynn hunched over, then Cindy stooped next to him, their shoulders touching.

Flynn felt her soft flesh, remembered the one dance they'd shared so many years ago. Then he took another turn and somehow they were tangled together on the slippery game mat.

As they bent, twisted, tangled, mangled, wound and curved, they were never more than inches apart. Inches that had once seemed like miles, he realized with sudden clarity. Because he had put them there.

The next call sent Cindy and Flynn falling, the kids bouncing on top of them. The game was over, but Flynn was slow to move away.

Cindy studied him curiously. "Are you ready for the cake and presents?"

He cleared his throat. "Sure." And he tried to clear his head. "Whatever you think is best."

She tilted her head. "Whatever *I* think is best?"

"Well, you did plan everything." He couldn't tell her she so distracted him that he could think of little else.

"Fine. Do you want to help me bring the cakes out?"

"Sure. I still can't believe you baked three cakes. And why are they such a secret?"

Her smile was mysterious. "You'll see."

Strangely he wanted to.

Cindy signaled to Katherine, who came to help them carry in the multiple trays that had been hidden away in the small butler's pantry behind the kitchen.

"What?" Flynn asked, staring at the unusual cakes.

"The shapes have a special meaning" was all Cindy would say. "You'll see why soon."

Flynn picked up the cake with Beth's name on it. Cindy and Katherine followed suit and soon all the cakes were positioned on their special tables. Cindy had loaded the kids' wagons with ice that held buckets of ice cream that could be pulled to each small table.

Cindy clapped her hands together. "It's time for cake and presents!"

Three cakes for the triplets on their third birthday. It couldn't be more perfect. At least when he figured out what the shapes meant, Flynn decided.

Candles lit, everyone began singing "Happy Birthday" with Noah and his friends playing in the background.

"Make a wish!" Cindy told the triplets as they pursed to blow out the candles.

"But don't tell what it is," Flynn added, suddenly remembering the few happy birthdays of his own childhood, memories he hadn't even realized were still stored within.

Beth's small face puckered in concentration. Mandy's eyes widened. And Alice looked dreamy.

Cindy glanced at Flynn, indicating it was up to him to tell them to blow out the candles.

"All together. Get ready, blow them out . . . now!"

The girls squealed as each of their tiny sets of candles expired and smoke whirled up from their cakes. Everyone clapped and cheered.

"I'll start getting the gifts," Cindy offered. "If you want to help them cut their cakes."

Flynn had a sudden memory of the girls' first birthday. Julia had organized the party, insisting on doing everything herself. When he'd offered to help cut the cake, she'd waved him away. Capable, he'd thought. But he also remembered the feeling of being excluded, as though his presence wasn't really needed.

Now, however, Cindy stood aside, allowing him to guide each girl's hand in slicing the first piece from each of their cakes.

Waiting until that very special moment was over and Katherine and Michael took over the cake-cutting chore, Cindy pulled out one gift apiece.

"Hold cake!" Beth demanded, pushing her plate at Flynn.

He smiled at her excitement as she ripped open Cindy's gift. It was a small ukelele. She studied it uncertainly.

"It's to play," Cindy explained. "Like when I make music on the piano."

Beth plucked one string, its twang startling all the triplets. As Mandy and Beth stared intently at the instrument, Cindy handed them each their presents.

Mandy unwrapped hers the fastest. "Music?" she asked, holding up a recorder.

Cindy nodded. "You blow into it."

Mandy did and was immediately delighted by the light woodwind sound the starter instrument produced.

Alice had her own present unwrapped by then, and she held up a small, child-size violin. "Alice music?"

Cindy produced a proportionately small bow. "You pull this over the strings."

Alice did and instead of the terrible yowling sound they expected, the child instinctively pulled the bow gently over the strings. Her face bloomed at the sound.

"That's wonderful!" Cindy exclaimed.

Pleased, but still shy, Alice glanced from the violin to her cake. "Matches!"

Flynn tore his gaze from his daughters to

their cakes. He had recognized the violin shape, but now he realized the other two were formed as a recorder and ukelele. Unexpectedly he grinned.

He could see that Alice's name was positioned on the frosting strings, as was Beth's. Mandy's lettering wove in between the recorder's apertures. Each was as unique as his daughters.

Glancing up, he caught Cindy's gaze on him. In it he saw a questioning, as though looking for his approval. He hadn't ever suspected she sought approval, instead acting on her own whims and wishes.

Still she'd done all this on her own for the girls, creating, working . . . and at the same time making him feel a part of things, rather than a bystander. He raised his hand in a thumbs-up gesture.

The bizarre makeup emphasized her wide grin. Irrationally he wondered how she could look so pretty, clown makeup and all.

Chapter Eleven

†

Flynn told himself that flying Cindy to dinner in San Antonio was a simple thank-you, nothing more. His plane was hangared in the small local airport that was used primarily for crop dusters and rich oil executives who vacationed in the privacy of the Hill Country. He hadn't expected Cindy to enjoy the mode of transportation; it was simply for expediency when he didn't have the time to drive. Usually he preferred to have his own car, especially in Houston. The commute from the airport to downtown took nearly as long as the drive from Rosewood and wasn't nearly as pleasant.

So it surprised him when Cindy's face lit up at the invitation, then further brightened when he mentioned the plane. Julia had hated his Cessna Skyhawk. He had finally talked her into going up once, but she'd hated every moment, scarcely able to bear it until he'd landed. Then she'd scrambled out, swearing never to get into his plane again. What, she had asked, would happen to the girls if they were both killed in a crash?

Now, as Flynn taxied down the narrow runway, he could scarcely believe the excitement in Cindy's expression. Leaning forward so far that she strained the straps of her seat belt, she stared out the windows.

Building up speed, Flynn took a moment to glance at Cindy. Instantly he recognized the pure adrenaline. The own rush he felt each time he jockeyed into the air.

With a gentle bump and swish, they were off the ground, gaining altitude.

"We're up!" Cindy exclaimed, still peering through the windshield. "This is so cool. Look!" she pointed. "It's like being in *Land of the Giants*. We can see the roofs and the *tiny* people!"

"You've been on a plane before," he commented in mild amusement.

"But not this kind. It's like a ride at Disneyland, only a whole lot better. In a commercial jet, you don't see the details. You get too high up too soon." She leaned even closer to the window, pulling her seat belt to its limit. "Look! Look! You can see the playground!" She laughed aloud. "If I had a plane like this, I'd be up here every day."

"I used to, a long time ago," Flynn admitted. "But not in the last few years."

She tore her attention from the fast-disappearing panorama below. "Why did you stop?"

"Julia didn't like it. She hated being in the plane herself, then worried every time I went up. So I only used it for business."

Cindy's eyes deepened in sympathetic understanding. "I know she felt that way. I didn't realize you'd cut back so much. Julia didn't mention that — only the concern. The way Mom and Dad died in that boating accident — it was tragic, but it changed Julia. She'd always been reserved, but after that, she absolutely detested anything that could even remotely be considered unsafe. She gave up horseback riding, boating, even biking." Cindy paused. "I worried because it was as though she wanted to create this impenetrable shell of safety. I felt she was afraid to have any fun, to really enjoy life because of her fear." Hesitating again, the tone of her voice cracked a bit. "And then to die so young from something she couldn't protect herself from. I don't know . . . it seemed so cruelly ironic."

Flynn nodded. "I agree. But I'm surprised you see it that way. After all, don't you believe your God could have saved her?"

Pain darkened her eyes, a deep abiding pain. "I won't pretend to understand every-

202

thing He does. But that's why it's called faith."

Flynn took a deep breath. "I don't want to ruin the afternoon. Maybe we should change the subject."

She glanced through the large windshield at the decidedly blue sky, the uncluttered white of the drifting clouds. "We can, but it's all around us."

They rode quietly for a while, then Cindy began to pick out landmarks below, her excitement rekindled, growing by the minute. As they approached the city, she pointed out the Tower of the Americas, a tall needlelike structure that had been erected in the sixties for the Hemisfair. San Antonio was a city of landmarks, historic and new. They flew over old missions, a new stadium and the curving river that defined San Antonio's image.

When they landed, then exited the plane, Cindy was still pumped. "If I were you, I'd fly every day." Her eyes widened. "We could fly to the monthly board meetings in Houston instead of driving, couldn't we?"

Amazed, Flynn stared at her. How could two sisters be so different? "You'd really want to do that?"

"Are you kidding? I'd ask you to fly me to the grocery store every day if there was a landing strip on Main Street."

His laughter erupted on its own again. Before he'd moved to Rosewood, that had been such a rare action it was almost nonexistent. "I've rented a car. We can pick it up and head downtown."

As they drove through the crowded streets, Cindy sadly noted the tall skyscrapers that surrounded the most famous of the city's landmarks. Built as a mission, the Alamo was the shrine of Texas independence.

"Do you know that when I was a little kid, I think I was about five, my parents brought us to see the Alamo. At that time, it stood all alone, no other buildings around it. I remember thinking it must be the biggest, most magnificent building in the world." She pointed to the mall and office structures that now dwarfed the symbol of the Lone Star state. "It seems sad somehow that all this commercialism has ruined that. When I toured the mission for the first time, the man in charge told us it was a shrine and cautioned us to be quiet. It was easy because there couldn't have been more than a dozen people inside. The last time I tried to visit the Alamo, hundreds of people were squeezed inside, so many that you couldn't even move. Again, the man outside gave the same instructions. Why I'm not sure, because once we were inside, with that many people there was more pandemonium than I imagine they had during the actual last days of the Alamo. I could have cried for what was lost, what would never be again."

Flynn could understand exactly how she felt, he'd had similar experiences. But the vision of Cindy crying over a lost historical landmark moved him beyond measure. Again, he wondered, who was this mercurial woman?

When he didn't comment, she angled her face. "Gives a new meaning to 'Remember the Alamo' though, doesn't it?"

"Tell you what. I know the Riverwalk's changed, but at least the river's still there. You game?"

She sighed, a purely feminine response. "I have to warn you, once I get there, you may have to drag me away."

"I'll chance it."

After parking the car, they crossed the street. Reaching a stairwell, they descended the stone steps. The famed Riverwalk, nestled below street level, lent European character to the distinctively Texas town. People were drawn to the "Venice of Texas" because it was the thread of the historical tapestry that was San Antonio. Deep roots of Spanish, Mexican and German heritage made the town unique and ripe with charm.

The Riverwalk wasn't as crowded as it would be in the coming summer days. Still, couples strolled the old riverbank. Once a secluded, little-known area, it was now a tourist mecca with sidewalk cafés, boutiques, gift shops and galleries. "As long as we're reminiscing, I can remember when there was only one restaurant on the Riverwalk."

"The Casa Rio near the stairs at the end of the sidewalk that goes up to Commerce Street," Cindy agreed. "The oldest restaurant on the Riverwalk."

"You've been there?" he asked in surprise.

"My dad brought me here. I was the one who loved traveling, so I went along when Mom and Julia wanted to stay home. He and I visited La Villita. Back then it was more authentic, not just touristy, and we watched the old glassblower. I remember wondering how he could blow that fiery glass all day, especially when it was so hot outside, but then he blew the most beautiful clear glass ship. And my dad bought it for me. I know it's silly, but I believed that with that ship as my good-luck piece, I could sail around the world."

"The one in your curio cabinet," Flynn suddenly remembered. "It's on a shelf by itself, right at eye level."

She nodded. "I'm surprised you remember."

"It's an unusual talisman," he replied.

"I suppose so." Cindy sighed. "After Mom and Dad passed away, Julia couldn't stand to look at it, so I packed the ship away and didn't take it out until I moved to Rosewood."

Flynn suddenly wondered why they'd all tiptoed around Julia. Probably because she was so delicate, so seemingly fragile. Her own trepidation had made them capitulate to her needs, he realized. Not because she wanted to manipulate them, but because she could never escape the fear.

And that he understood. Fear, even one as old as his own, never disappeared. It always lurked around the edges, threatening to erupt, to maim again. Yet Cindy hadn't shared the insecurity with Julia.

"How is it you escaped all the pain Julia felt?"

Cindy's eyes filled with wisdom and acceptance. "I didn't. But I learned to deal with it instead of hiding, and that's being truthful rather than critical. It's not as though Julia wanted to be frightened. But for me, I felt I'd faced the worst I ever could. I found comfort in my faith, but Julia had a harder time accepting God's will."

Flynn frowned. "Julia didn't even go to church."

"She used to. Even though she still agonized over losing Mom and Dad, she was still attending until she met you."

Shocked, Flynn stared at her. "That can't be true."

Cindy shrugged. "You offered her security, safety, stability. She thought she needed that more at the time."

"Doesn't say much for me, does it?" he asked wryly.

"Oh, I didn't mean that! Julia loved you."

Maybe so. And maybe she really had only needed what he had to offer. But Flynn put the thoughts out of his mind as they climbed the steps, paused at the arches that crossed over the river, looking down into the water, the slow-moving boats. The Arneson River Theater still remained on the now fully developed Riverwalk. Once the amphitheater had been one of only a handful of structures.

Despite the commercialization of the quaint spot, it was still incredibly romantic. As evening approached, lights hung up and down the banks illuminated, strings of fairy lights that twinkled over the brackish water.

"There's nothing like dusk on Paseo del Rio," Cindy murmured, using the Spanish name for the Riverwalk.

He glanced at Cindy, seeing the reflection of the lights on her brilliant hair and sparkling eyes. "No, there's not."

By mutual accord, they strolled to the end of the walk, seeking out the restaurant they'd been to as children. They were escorted to a table beside the water.

"It looks just like it did when I was five," Cindy marveled. "Busier, of course. But unchanged."

It was a new memory, Flynn thought without warning. One they didn't share with Julia. Only each other and a good part of their pasts. And that was remarkable for him.

As they had only a few times since Flynn's move to Rosewood, they enjoyed a few hours unaffected by what usually lay between them. The food was as they'd remembered, but the conversation wasn't.

Flynn admitted that he still wasn't sure about the move to Rosewood, also admitted that it had been made reluctantly.

And Cindy finally confessed that she still wondered why he'd made the choice, that it made her distrustful.

They were huge confessions for two such guarded people. But the admissions allowed some of the tension between them to dissipate.

Cindy's finger rimmed the moisture that formed on her glass of iced tea. "Thanks for bringing me here, Flynn. I've loved everything — the flight, bringing back old memories, even my enchiladas."

He had, too. But it wasn't in Flynn to admit that. "I wanted to say thank you. For the girls' birthday party, taking us in, everything."

She shrugged. "There's no need to thank me. I did it because I wanted to. That's why I work with my Rainbow kids. They give me back so much more than I can do for them."

"You never told me how you got into that."

Explaining, Cindy's face took on that rare softness he'd glimpsed, but when she spoke of what she would do to protect them, she grew equally fierce.

"Isn't it kind of unusual for a church to take on a project like that?" Flynn questioned.

"I'm not really sure," Cindy replied. "I was the one who formed the group, with the kids I just told you about. They're kids who need extra care and attention for more reasons than I can name. The church just lets me use space in the Sunday school building."

"This was *your* idea?"

"Yeah. The kids needed someone. I had lots of time and energy to give."

"Still . . ."

"Why me?" she asked wryly. "Doesn't fit your picture of me, does it?"

Nothing did anymore. "It just seems like a lot for one woman to tackle."

"No one else was stepping up to bat."

"But why you?"

She smiled. "Because it was the right thing to do."

He stared at her in silence, a thousand questions begging to be voiced. Instead he asked the waiter for the bill. Once he'd settled it, they strolled back down the sidewalk, watching boats gliding by, hearing the gentle slosh of the water as it lapped against the riverbank.

Angling his head, he saw the wistfulness on Cindy's face as she looked at the boats. "Why don't we take a ride on one?"

Her smile surfaced. "Do we have time?"

"You're the one who made the arrangements for the girls with Katherine. Do you think she'd mind if we're about an hour later?"

Grin widening, she shook her head, pulling a cell phone from a side pocket in her purse. "We can call and let her know."

Cindy quickly phoned Katherine as they entered the short line for the next boat, and soon were on board. Since it was still late spring, a cool breeze skipped through the air, disguising the hot, humid days of summer that were just ahead.

The San Antonio River wound through the business district of the town, criss-crossed by quaint curved bridges, the banks beautifully landscaped with native plants.

The ride down the river was near magical, the strings of tiny white lights providing a romantic, winsome background. Over-hanging tree branches reached out across the river, teasing but not quite touching the passing boats. Another new memory, Flynn realized. One as unexpected as the first.

Glancing over, he saw Cindy's gaze on his. But seeing him, she looked away, her porcelain skin pale against the deepening night. So different, he thought again. But this time it wasn't a disquieting thought, rather one that intrigued.

Water continued to lap against the sides of the boat, a gentle thrumming that echoed beneath the overhanging walkways, one that whispered to his thoughts.

It seemed the ride ended too quickly. Flynn was reluctant as he stepped from the boat. The allure of the surroundings made him want to take Cindy's hand, to linger, to discover more.

But her expression was rueful as she glanced at her watch. "Katherine will be expecting us soon."

It was ridiculous to be so disappointed. It was only a thank-you dinner, he reminded himself. Yet the thoughts that had begun on the boat echoed as they flew home.

It wasn't a long flight, yet the plane was incredibly intimate in the dark night.

"The lights from the homes and buildings look so snug and cozy, secured for the night," Cindy said softly. "I love that feeling, that all's right with the world."

Flynn's voice was quiet, not wanting to provoke the unique moment. "But you can't know that."

"No, but I can hope it's true."

He glanced over at her. "I suppose so," he replied, settling for the words even though *hope* hadn't been in his own vocabulary for many years. The clear night sky stretched out before them, the evening darkening, the wonder growing.

Chapter Twelve

†

Nearly three weeks later, Cindy still thought often of their evening in San Antonio, the unspoken repercussions. She and Flynn had shared an uneasy truce since then, but Cindy held no illusions. Nearly every day Flynn went to the construction site of the house he was building. It seemed to her that he wanted to leave her house as soon as possible.

Before he did though, she wanted to be sure the girls had a good religious foundation. Thus every afternoon, like today, she blended songs and stories with a biblical theme into their music lesson time.

Cindy was thrilled that the triplets were still excited about the instruments she had given them. She had taught them some basic notes, which they practiced faithfully. Using her own methods, Cindy picked out simple notes on the piano while the girls followed along. Now they played often in the evenings and also with the Rainbow class.

"The Jesus song," Mandy requested, her shorthand version of "Jesus Loves Me."

When they finished the song, Cindy

clapped her hands. "That was wonderful! When your mommy and I were little girls that was our favorite song."

Beth screwed her always inquisitive face into a question mark. "Where's my mommy?"

Although both she and Flynn had tried to explain this before, it was too much for the children to understand. "You know what, there's a book that I'd like to read to you, about a little girl."

She read them the story of a young girl whose mother had died. The girl looked and looked everywhere for her mother and asked everyone she met where her mother was. But no one knew. Until she went to church.

"Was she there?" Beth asked.

"No, but that's when she learned her mommy had gone to Heaven. Just like your mommy."

"Is it nice there?" Mandy asked.

"Yes, because all the people your mommy loved were there, waiting to greet her. She'd missed her mommy and daddy, too, and was very happy to see them." Cindy's eyes misted, her own longing for her lost family never completely at bay.

"Did they hug her?" Alice asked, concern in her tiny face.

"So much, it probably shook up a storm," Cindy replied, smiling at the image.

"I'm happy Mommy's in heaven," Beth finally concluded.

Still smiling, Cindy glanced up. But her happy expression drained away as she encountered Flynn's furious face. He must have come in while she had been absorbed in telling the story. "Flynn," she greeted him quietly.

"Mommy's in heaven," Mandy told him with cheerful confidence.

"You girls go into the kitchen and get an apple," Flynn told them with quiet authority.

"No more story?" Beth asked.

"No," Flynn replied tightly. "No more stories."

Once the girls were out of earshot, Flynn advanced. "What was that about?"

"They wanted to know where their mother is."

"In the ground," Flynn replied, with barely controlled anger.

And something deep, deep inside Cindy fractured. It no longer mattered if Flynn didn't return her love, couldn't see the person she now was. His lack of faith was even more painful than unrequited love. And something she could never, never compromise on. So she kept her silence.

"I thought I'd made myself clear. Don't interfere with my children's beliefs."

"You *want* them to believe their mother is in the ground? That they have no possible hope of being reunited with her?"

"You've crossed the line."

Cindy set her teeth, trying to restrain her own temper.

"I thought your Sunday school thing was strictly social. Since it's not, that's out."

Shocked, she stared at him. "You can't mean that!"

"I've never been more sure of anything. You seem to keep forgetting that *I'm* their parent."

"That's where you're wrong. I've never lost sight of that fact. But I think you have."

The following days were so tense, Cindy considered going away for a while, leaving the house to Flynn. Then one of the girls would climb in her lap, and her resolve fled.

The rest of the week passed and when Sunday morning arrived, Cindy dressed for church. Once downstairs in the kitchen, she picked up her purse.

"Us go?" Beth asked, starting to scramble from her booster seat.

"Not today," Flynn answered for her.

"Sunny school?" Mandy asked, seeing that Cindy was holding her Bible, as well.

Cindy glanced at Flynn, then nodded.

"I wanna go!" Beth wailed.

Alice and Mandy also tried to climb down from their booster seats. "Wait for us, Cinny!"

"You'll have to talk to your daddy," Cindy replied, pain wiping the color from her face.

Feeling as though she were betraying her sister, Cindy turned and fled. But before she could escape through the front door, she heard the girls' voices rising in demand, then the beginning of sniffling cries. Cindy pressed her head against the door as she heard the cries increase to sobs.

Pulling back, it took all of her power to walk through the door, to not turn back around, confront Flynn and console the girls. But this was Flynn's decision. Girding her strength, Cindy made her way to church, knowing she needed His help now more than ever.

Six days later, Flynn rubbed at the throbbing headache that had centered between his brows. He'd thought the previous Sunday had been bad with the girls crying and throwing tantrums because they

218

wanted to go with Cindy to church. But the rest of the week was even worse. Every morning before work and each evening when he returned, the girls were at him, pleading to go back to "Sunny school."

Flynn had been certain they would forget all about it within a day, two at the most. But they hadn't forgotten. They repeated over and over again that they wanted to sing, and hear stories, and color and see their friends.

Now he was facing another Sunday morning of forcing the children to remain behind as they watched Cindy leave for church.

Picking up a bottle of aspirin, he quickly swallowed two, washing them down with one of Cindy's organic juice blends.

He had two choices. He could insist on having things his way and create another round of chaos. Or he could let the girls attend church while they stayed with Cindy, then when they moved into their own house, he could let the habit fade away on its own.

It was his decision.

He pictured the onslaught of three pairs of eyes, ones that had been boring into him all week. And he knew he couldn't withstand them any longer.

Knowing the girls were napping, Flynn sought out Cindy, guessing she had retreated to the quiet of the backyard. She had made a point of being anywhere he wasn't the entire week.

He was right. She was in the far corner of the yard, alternately weeding the flower bed and stretching her hand between two loose boards in the fence to pet the neighbor's dog.

Dispensing with small talk, he resisted the urge to rub at his throbbing forehead. "I've come to a decision."

"Another one?"

He winced. She was still stubborn, still challenging. There was no bending, no complacency. Nothing except her incredible appeal to suggest she was the weaker sex. "While we are staying here, the girls can go with you to church."

She turned around so that she could see him. "And afterward?"

"What difference does that make? They're my children. I'll do what I think is best for them."

"No, actually you're doing what you think is best for you."

Flynn stopped short of throwing his hands in the air. "You can't just win, can you? You have to win *and* have the last word."

But there was no victory in her expression. Only sadness colored her brilliant green eyes. "You just don't get it. Neither one of us wins."

For a moment, Flynn could only stare at her. But he couldn't believe that was true. He had dedicated himself to protecting his daughters, ensuring they would never suffer as he had. "It's up to you, then," he said finally.

"No," she replied, her voice shaking. "This is your decision. I'll take them with me in the morning only if you've told them they can go."

Flynn turned away, unwilling to search her eyes again. That was far too painful. And equally hopeless.

Once inside the house, Flynn kept himself busy, going over some revised plans for the new house. He had an urgent need to finish the house, to move away from all the confusion he'd felt since staying in Cindy's home. Closing his eyes, he could picture the disappointment in Cindy's expression, the certainty that she disapproved.

It wasn't up to her to approve or disapprove, he told himself righteously. Glancing toward the stairs, he thought of his innocent daughters still asleep. He would do anything to protect them, anything. And that's what Cindy didn't understand. He wasn't keeping them from church to deprive them, rather to save them from the hurt he'd known. And now Cindy had put him in an untenable position. Hurt them by denying their attendance, or hurt them by letting them believe a delusion that could only lead to disappointment.

They were only three, Flynn reminded himself. Young enough to forget once they were in their own home. Glancing around, Flynn looked at the comfortable, cozy space Cindy had created. The girls would miss this, he realized. And in their young lives they'd been forced to miss too much already.

With leaden feet he stepped on the first riser. It was time to wake the girls. Time to tell them that he wouldn't force this particular sacrifice right now, that they could go to church with "Cinny" in the morning.

But he made a second resolution, as well. From now on, he'd spend less time at his new office and more time with his girls. Because it had been easy, he'd allowed Cindy too much influence on them. It was time he took that back. Before it was too late.

In the following weeks, Cindy had taken an inventory of her own, as well. But before she could act on it, crisis struck.

One day she had gone to pick up Ricky for Rainbow class and had found an ambulance parked in front of the house. The young boy was crying as they loaded his mother into the ambulance.

Sweeping the child into her embrace, Cindy put him in her car, following the ambulance to the hospital. Using her cell phone, she alerted Katherine who promised to take the class for the day.

Once at the hospital, Cindy held Ricky's hand as the doctors worked on his mother. The child clung to Cindy, terrified.

And when the doctor emerged from the room, his face was somber.

No, Cindy prayed. *Don't take this child's only parent.*

"I'm sorry," the doctor began, looking first at Cindy, then down at young Ricky. "We knew it was inevitable. But we did try everything."

"My mommy?" Ricky asked in a wavering voice.

Cindy knelt beside him, still clasping his hands. "Mommy's in Heaven now with Jesus."

"But I want her here with me!" Ricky shouted. "Not with Jesus!"

The tears came then, huge gulping sobs.

Cindy pulled him close, holding his shaking body next to her, feeling her own tears wetting her cheeks, salting her lips. While they both cried for what Ricky had lost and could never regain, the doctor quietly moved away.

As Cindy smoothed the hair back from his forehead and searched her pocket for a tissue, Ricky finally spoke. "Why did she have to die?"

Cindy searched for the right words, but couldn't find them. "I don't know. She just got very sick."

"Did she want to go to Heaven?"

Cindy felt her own heart breaking. "She didn't want to leave you, but now her pain is all gone."

"She won't take no more pills?"

"No more."

"She couldn't breathe sometimes," Ricky admitted, the tears thickening his young voice. "And she hurted."

"Well, she doesn't hurt anymore."

Ricky nodded, then looked up again. "Where will I go, Miss Cindy?" His face crumpled. "I don't have nobody."

And in that instant, she made another binding and final decision. "Yes, you do. You have me. You'll come and live with me."

Tears still ran down his cheeks, wetting his T-shirt. "For how long?"

Forever, she thought to herself, if it was within her power. "For as long as you can. I think your mother would like that."

He glanced back at the room that held his mother's still body. Again his mouth trembled. "Mommy said you were the nicest lady she ever knew."

Cindy's own tears started again. "And your mother raised the nicest little boy in the world." Clasping his hand, she led them down the hall.

Speaking quietly and briefly with the doctor, Cindy told them she was taking Ricky home with her and to notify the mortuary that she would be paying for the funeral.

Once back at her house, Katherine met her at the front door, having made sure the kids were playing out back, rather than inside.

Cindy knelt beside Ricky one more time. "I have to make some phone calls. Can you stay with Miss Katherine for a few minutes?"

Ricky didn't want to release her hand, but finally nodded.

Katherine picked up his other hand. "Let's have a glass of milk, okay? Miss

Donna, one of the Sunday school teachers, and the other kids are in the yard and we can stay inside if you'd like."

Again Ricky nodded, the motion wobbly and uncertain.

Katherine hugged him close, as well.

Cindy met her friend's gaze, signaling her gratitude, before disappearing into the privacy of the conservatory. Quickly she called her attorney, who promised to notify child services and file an immediate petition for temporary custody along with her request for permanent adoption.

Then he hesitated. "Are you certain about this, Cindy? Permanent adoption?"

"Very certain," she replied without hesitation. "Can you let me know if there's any problem with the immediate permission to keep him?"

"I don't anticipate any since there are no relatives. It was wise of you to investigate the family situation while his mother was alive and could give you the information, dismal as it is." He hesitated. "This is a lot to take on, Cindy."

"Not as much as a six-year-old who's just lost his last living family member."

The attorney rang off and Cindy contacted the mortuary, verifying that she was paying for the funeral, also requesting that everything be elegant but tasteful.

Drained, Cindy sat back in her chair, her heart breaking for this small child.

Hearing a noise at the doorway, she glanced up, meeting Flynn's curious expression. True to the resolve he'd informed her of, Flynn had been returning home from work in the early afternoons, determined to be a bigger part of the triplets' upbringing.

"Why is it so quiet?" he asked, entering the room.

She didn't answer at first.

Flynn's own expression turned downward as he examined her pale face. "Has there been an accident? Are the girls all right? Are —"

"They're fine," she said finally, her voice as low as her spirits.

"Then what is it?"

"Ricky Dunn's mother died today."

Flynn drew his brows together. "The little kid in your class that's always stirring something up?"

"Yes, that would be him."

"Tough break," Flynn sympathized. "Did you cancel the class today out of respect?"

She shook her head. "The kids are in the backyard. Katherine and Donna took over."

"Oh. Well, I can see why it'd be hard for you today."

She met his gaze. "That's not the reason." Briefly she explained how she'd come to be at Ricky's house, then the hospital.

"Where is he now?" Flynn questioned. "With the grandparents?"

Again she shook her head. "He's remarkably like you and me, Flynn. He has no other family."

Shocked, he stared at her. "This little kid doesn't have *anybody?*"

"Not exactly. He has me."

"Well, that's fine on a temporary basis —"

"You don't understand, Flynn. It's not temporary."

"You're taking this child in to raise?"

She nodded. "He needs me."

"You plan on taking in every other orphan in the state?"

"I probably would if it were possible. But I don't know them as I do Ricky. And I won't let him grow up without a single person to watch out for him."

Flynn drew his brows together. "You mean you're going to adopt him?"

"What would you have me do, Flynn? Turn him over to strangers who don't care about him? A child who just lost the mother he cherished, and who has no one else?"

"Well, no, but you've never had kids of your own and —"

She ignored the sharp if unintentional barb of his comment. "Maybe not. But this isn't a game to me, Flynn. I know you still see me as a scatterbrained twenty-one-year-old with thoughts of only parties and fun. Well, yes, I did like parties and I did like having fun. But that wasn't all there was to me then. And it certainly isn't all there is to me now. I intend to give this wonderful little boy a home. I'm raw, knowing the pain he's suffering, but I'm also grateful I can be here for him now, that the Lord gave me this opportunity."

Confusion settled over the surprise in his face. "You really see it that way? As an opportunity?"

"Yes," she replied quietly. "I do. Flynn, we've both known our share of loss, we know how it feels to be the one left behind. Can you imagine how it would be if you were only a child?"

He blanched, something Cindy had never seen, not even at Julia's funeral.

"Flynn?"

Pulling himself back to the moment, he met her gaze. "Yes, maybe I can. Where's Ricky now?"

"In the kitchen with Katherine." She

glanced down at the phone. "I wanted to be alone while I talked to my lawyer and then the funeral home."

He nodded. "Do you want me to clear the girls out for a while? I could take them to Houston for a visit, let you have some space."

Knowing the offer was sincere, she felt only gratitude despite its misplaced intent. "No. Actually, I think it would be good for Ricky to have them around. He already feels so alone."

Flynn again looked at her questioningly. "What happened to his father? Were they divorced?"

"No. He died when Ricky was a baby."

Unconsciously, Flynn winced. "And you're sure there aren't any grandparents?"

"All gone. His father had one sister who died in childhood. His mother was an only child. You know the equation, Flynn. It's just like our own."

Flynn glanced in the direction of the kitchen, even though it couldn't be seen from the confines of the conservatory. "How old did you say he was?"

"Six."

For a moment Flynn's jaw worked. Then he nodded.

And silence stood between them for

several long moments.

Flynn lifted his head at last. "What can I do to help?"

Unbelievably touched, Cindy couldn't stop the tears that suddenly erupted, the trembling of her lips. Blinded by the onslaught, she didn't see Flynn walk around the library table until he stood in front of her. Then his arms were around her, holding her close, offering the comfort she hadn't experienced since before the loss of her parents.

The stiffness of her shock cracked as she laid her head on Flynn's sturdy shoulder and let the tears flow. Tears for all their losses. Things that could never be made right again.

Flynn's hand was gentle as he stroked the back of her head, and for just the moment she gave in to the need to remain like that, buffeted from all the pain that was ahead. Pain made worse by the fact that he couldn't shelter her from the biggest loss, that of his love. And again she issued the same silent prayer she had been repeating for weeks, that the Lord would soften Flynn's heart and show him the path back to his faith.

Chapter Thirteen

✝

Determined to keep his promise, in the following weeks Flynn often returned home by late afternoon to see his daughters and Ricky. He had hired six more employees to keep up with the growth of the business. Within little more than a month, their volume had quadrupled.

He had resolved to devote more time to the kids than to his software development business. And now it weighed on him that he had the responsibilities of both work and family. Due to Rosewood's stagnant job market, the positions he had offered meant life-altering changes to his new employees. If he dropped the ball, it wasn't just a financial loss for him; it could harm the people he'd hired, people who had placed their trust in him. He knew two had already purchased small homes, based on their new earnings. And Flynn couldn't live with himself if they lost their homes due to his negligence.

Which put him squarely in the middle again.

But this afternoon, he'd been able to leave early, reaching the house just after four o'clock. He could hear the babble of young voices coming from the backyard. Cindy's Rainbow kids. He couldn't believe she was insisting on keeping both classes intact, but she said these emotionally scarred children needed her. Flynn had argued that she was stretching her energies in too many directions: Ricky, the triplets, the Rainbow kids. But Cindy wouldn't budge.

Stepping through the French doors, he was appalled to see Mandy crying, sprawled out on the terrace, blood gushing from her mouth. With a cloth grasped in one hand, Cindy was holding the child's head.

Fear had Flynn beside his daughter in mere seconds. "What happened?"

"The kids got a little rambunctious," Cindy explained, pressing the cloth gently around Mandy's mouth.

"Rambunctious?" he demanded. "What's that supposed to mean?"

"They were running, Paul pushed her a little and she fell."

Fury nearly blinded him; still Flynn reached for his daughter, intending to pick her up. "I knew something like this would happen."

Cindy laid a restraining hand on his arm.

"What are you doing?"

"Taking her to the hospital, of course!"

"Flynn, you're overreacting. One of her teeth poked her lip when she fell. It's not serious."

He motioned to Mandy's swollen mouth and the blood that had dripped on her T-shirt. "It looks pretty serious to me!"

"Flynn, have you ever seen one of the girls bleeding before?"

"No . . . Why?"

"Because the first time it's terrifying. But trust me, she's okay. We'll put some ice on it to stop the swelling, and see, Mandy's already stopped crying."

Flynn studied his daughter's face, seeing her tears had indeed stopped. "Still, better safe than sorry."

Cindy kept her tone mild. "Taking her to the hospital would be pretty scary. And the bleeding's almost stopped."

But Flynn hadn't spent his store of protective impulses. "I knew that letting them run around in jeans wasn't a good idea."

Cindy didn't rise to the bait, instead widening her eyes in mild disbelief. "She'd still have fallen if she'd been wearing a dress. And then she'd also have scraped knees."

"If you hadn't insisted on bringing these ragamuffins into your house . . ." Flynn began, but the words trailed away as he watched her face transform to one of wounded incredulity.

"It's good to know how you really feel," she said in a tone that was as quiet as it was livid. "Before Ricky discovered it the hard way."

Flynn wished he could bite back the words. "I didn't mean him."

"No? Then which particular *ragamuffin* were you referring to? They're all either scarred emotionally or in desperate need of nurturing. Take your pick."

Flynn passed a hand over his forehead, then glanced down at Mandy. "I think we'd better discuss this later."

Cindy thrust the moist cloth at him. "Be sure to wrap the ice in this or it will burn her skin."

"Cinny!" Mandy wailed when Cindy rose.

Flynn met Cindy's determined gaze, then watched as her eyes closed briefly.

Then she held out a hand to Mandy. "Let's go in the kitchen. We'll show Daddy how to fix the booboo, okay?"

Trailing her, Flynn knew he'd been given one last reprieve. Glancing into the yard, and catching sight of sad-looking little Ricky, Flynn knew he had to make good on this final chance.

★ ★ ★

Cindy watched as the sun surrendered to the far horizon. It never ceased to amaze her, this show the Lord provided them on a daily basis, its beauty never matched by even the most talented artists over the centuries.

Night sounds began as darkness tried to slip past twilight's final barriers. It was that indeterminate time of day, not daylight, yet not dark. A calm time of day, Cindy always thought, one that bordered between the worries of day and the loneliness of night.

The sounds of crickets and baritone bullfrogs were equally comforting. She needed this sameness in her life. As much as she craved adventure, she was deeply rooted to this community, to the things in her life that had become so important.

Things Flynn Mallory would never understand.

She was glad the triplets were safely tucked in bed, the crisis over Mandy's minor injury past. Having agreed to let Ricky lose himself with the PlayStation game in the sitting room off the kitchen, she kept track of the time, not wanting him to be left on his own. Flynn was in the house, but that wasn't a particular comfort.

And to think she'd believed his offer to

help with young Ricky. Then again, she had always believed her white knight would eventually find her, as well.

Hearing footsteps on the terrace, she turned, wondering if she'd miscalculated the time. To her surprise, Flynn and Ricky were walking outside together.

As she watched, Flynn was clearly not at ease, yet he sat with Ricky at the old wrought-iron table. From her spot deep in the back of the yard, Cindy couldn't hear their conversation, but she could see the look of concern on Flynn's face, one that also seemed beset by some unknown pain. And again she wondered about the mystery who was Flynn Mallory.

She watched them for the next hour, sensing that Flynn was trying to draw out the boy. Ricky had been terribly quiet since he'd come to their home, his grieving a visible thing.

For days after the funeral, he'd hardly spoken. It had surprised Cindy when Flynn had attended Mrs. Dunn's funeral with them. But he'd stood solidly beside Cindy and Ricky. And she was sure that the service had brought a wash of unwelcome memories, yet Flynn had remained stoic. Cindy had been the one to put Ricky on her lap, then comfort him through the painful service. But she had appreciated Flynn's silent show of support.

She'd thought it meant he had a genuine change of heart, that perhaps her prayers were working. But then this afternoon . . .

Now she wondered again. Did Flynn have two sides that battled for dominance? One that shut out compassion, and one that offered it? Or was she still a lovesick girl who couldn't get a grip on her own heart?

The questions haunted her for days as she watched Flynn with Ricky. First he'd brought home a soccer ball and net to practice kicking. Then he'd asked Cindy if he could sign the boy up for the soccer team. She'd commented that since it was late spring, there was only a month left of the sport. But that didn't faze Flynn, who told her that they could sign up for Little League to fill the summer days.

It confused her in many ways. Because this wasn't an instant bonding. In fact, the more Flynn offered to do for Ricky, the more tortured he appeared. Flynn's appetite had lessened to the point that Cindy urged him to eat hamburgers and French fries, but he insisted he just wasn't hungry. His face grew more gaunt. And each time when he thought no one was looking, he studied Ricky as though watching a ghost.

After this went on for two weeks Cindy decided it was time to confront Flynn. She chose the one time she knew they would be alone — as they traveled to the board meeting in Houston.

Although Cindy continued to love the sensation of flying in the small plane, this time she didn't marvel about it. And she guessed that discussing Flynn's past wouldn't be wise while he was piloting the plane.

After the meeting concluded, Flynn asked where she wanted to have lunch. But a crowded restaurant wasn't what Cindy had in mind.

"Why don't we walk for a while?" she asked.

They strolled along the sidewalks, filled with rushing pedestrians. Cindy glanced up at Antioch Baptist, the city's oldest black Protestant church. It sat between half a dozen mammoth structures, yet it wasn't dwarfed by any of them, instead remaining the most beautiful building in the circular street's crown. Its grace reinforced her resolve.

"Let's head toward Sam Houston Park," she suggested. "It's just a block away."

"Fine," Flynn agreed.

The park was an oasis in the crowded city.

Although bordered by towering sky-scrapers, the park itself was tranquil, popu-lated only by historic buildings from the state's past that had been relocated to the one central spot.

A small store in the park, run by the Heri-tage Museum, sold sandwiches, chips, cookies and drinks. Flynn and Cindy pur-chased enough for a small, but substantial picnic.

Since it was nearly two o'clock, most of the downtown lunch crowd had dispersed. Cindy and Flynn found a bench that offered privacy.

She felt her nerves building as she waited to approach the subject. They were nearly finished with their sandwiches when she took the plunge. "Flynn?"

"Hmm?"

"I need to talk to you about something."

He seemed relaxed by the surroundings, and unaware of her nervousness. "Shoot."

"It's about Ricky."

"What about him?"

She swallowed. "I'm wondering why you offered to help me with him."

He hesitated, and for a moment she won-dered if he would answer. When he did, his voice was hoarse. "He reminds me of my brother."

Surprise nearly stilled her as well. "I didn't know you had a brother."

"I never talk about it. Todd died when he was six."

"Ricky's age," Cindy murmured.

Flynn nodded.

"Can you tell me what happened?"

This time his hesitation was much larger, less surmountable. "I don't think you want to hear it and I certainly don't want to dig back that far."

Earnestly she met his gaze. "I *do* want to know. I *need* to know, to understand. And if it's tormenting you this much, *you* need to talk about it."

For a long time Flynn didn't say anything, his eyes taking on a faraway expression. He gripped the remainder of his sandwich, unintentionally crushing it in his clenched hand.

And when he finally, reluctantly spoke, his voice was gruff. "My mother wasn't like any of my friends' mothers. She was always scattered in one direction or another, off on some new quest. I guess some people would call it an incurable zest for life. But it's hard to see it like that when you're a kid, watching out for your younger brother, and you find yourself standing in front of school, the rec center or the movies waiting for her,

241

realizing she had forgotten about us. Oh, she always showed up eventually, apologizing, explaining she'd been caught up in one thing or another." He laughed, a caustic, raw sound. "Something that interested her more than either Todd or me. Then she'd insist on buying ice cream cones or hot dogs to make it up to us. She'd laugh and cajole us into believing the makeup treat was far better than her timeliness. And it usually worked."

Cindy swallowed the sudden dryness in her throat, dreading what was to come. "And then?" she prompted gently.

"I was nine years old. I had a bad case of chicken pox so I was confined to bed with calamine lotion and comic books." Again Flynn hesitated, his jaw working. "Since I couldn't go to school and watch out for Todd, I made sure Mom left on time to pick him up. But on the way she detoured to a flea market. I guess she only planned to stop for only a few minutes. But, as usual, the time escaped her. When she realized she was more than an hour late to pick up Todd, she sped off toward the school." Flynn's voice thickened. "But Todd had gotten tired of waiting and I wasn't there to make sure he didn't wander away."

Bending his head, Flynn rubbed at his

forehead. "It wasn't too hard for Mom to find him. Flashing emergency lights lit up the street next to the school. Todd had walked in front of a car." Flynn swallowed as he raised his head, again staring hard at the same faraway place. "He was killed instantly."

Tears misted in Cindy's eyes as she reached for Flynn's empty hand. At first he didn't respond, his own hand rigid. Then he glanced back at Cindy, seeing the tears roll silently down her cheeks. Unfurling his hand, he took Cindy's. And the fragment of sandwich dropped unnoticed from the other.

"I'm so sorry, Flynn. That must have destroyed your family."

"It was the beginning."

Even more horrified, she gripped his hand more firmly. "The beginning?"

"Mom committed suicide the day after Todd's funeral. She took a handful of pills that my dad didn't know she'd gotten from the doctor . . . and never woke up."

Anguish sliced through her and she couldn't control the tears that continued wetting her cheeks. "Oh, Flynn. That must have been horrible for you."

"My dad did his best, but he was never the same. For all that was wrong about my mother, I guess she was the love of his life. By the time I was nineteen, he died of grief, a broken man."

Cindy couldn't find words of sympathy that didn't fall miles short of how she felt. Instead she wrapped her arms around him, pressing her tear-soaked cheek against his.

When they finally pulled away, Flynn looked at her with a bit of wonder. "I never even told Julia the whole story. She was already filled with so much of her own pain . . . well, it never seemed the right time."

"I'm glad you told me," she said softly, knowing it was true. "I remember when I first met you. Even though you were five years older than me, I remember thinking you seemed decades older in maturity. No wonder. You had to grow up when you were only nine."

"I never thought about it that way."

Cindy continued to hold his hand, offering her support. "It sounds as though even before Todd's accident, you were older than your years, watching out for him. Then I suspect you watched out for your father after your mother's death. That's an incredible amount of responsibility for such a young child."

He shrugged, clearly uncomfortable with the praise. "If I hadn't been home sick, if I'd been there for Todd —"

"Flynn! You were a small child yourself! And you couldn't help having chicken pox! Surely you can't have carried around that guilt all these years?"

"Some of it. Most of it rests on my mother's shoulders. She should have behaved like a responsible adult. Instead she valued fun more than her family. And look what happened. It destroyed everyone but me."

Cindy chewed on her bottom lip. "It's destroying you, too, bit by bit. Don't you see that, Flynn? You've carried this burden alone for too many years."

"And who do you suggest I give it to?" he asked bitterly. "I doubt there are many pack mules looking to take it on."

"I know you don't want to hear this, but you need the Lord to lean upon, to help you carry your pain."

"The same God that turned His back on us? Where was He when Todd was hit by that car? And when my mother swallowed a bottle of pills? And my father died of a broken heart? Where was He then, Cindy?"

But she knew that she didn't have the answers that he needed. Only the Lord did. And now she was even more uncertain whether Flynn could ever accept Him again.

Chapter Fourteen

†

A week later Flynn was hammering a backboard onto the pole he'd had installed beneath the large oak when he heard a car pull up. He glanced over to see who it was.

Noah Brady, dressed in an impeccable tux, stepped out of the sleek Porsche. Cindy had told him she would be out for the evening. She'd failed to mention it would be with Noah.

An untenable kernel of jealousy knotted his stomach, and Flynn turned back to the pole.

"Planning on a little basketball?" Noah asked as he approached.

Flynn shrugged. "The kids should like it."

"Yep. Hey, why don't you join the church team? We could use a decent player."

"I'm not much into church stuff."

Noah nodded. "Fair enough. But the invitation's open. We want to make you feel welcome."

"Because of Cindy?" Flynn asked tightly.

"Sure. We like to keep her happy."

"I bet you do," Flynn muttered beneath his breath.

"I'm sorry. I didn't catch that."

"Nothing." Flynn drove the final nail into the backboard. "Come on inside. I'll see if Cindy's ready."

"Thanks. I don't want to be late."

Flynn looked up and down Noah's formal wear. "Little early for going out on the town, isn't it?"

Noah laughed. "Good one."

Flynn had no idea what the other man meant by that, but led him inside anyway, by way of the back door.

His daughters were grouped around the table, Ricky keeping an eye on them. Flynn wanted the basketball hoop to be a surprise, so he'd invented an excuse for Ricky to watch the girls.

The triplets squealed with delight as they spotted Noah, begging for him to play the piano.

"Now *this* is the ideal audience," Noah replied with a wide grin. Then he glanced at Flynn. "Do you mind?"

Hiding his thoughts, Flynn shook his head. "No, go ahead." Quickly he stabbed the button on the intercom. "Cindy, Noah's here."

"Thanks!" she replied cheerily.

His good mood out the window, Flynn helped Ricky clean up the mess the girls had made with their watercolors.

"Are you mad?" Ricky asked.

Flynn withheld a sigh, immediately regretting causing the child more concern. "No. Just have a lot on my mind. You know, I was thinking a basketball hoop might be kind of fun."

Ricky's always saddened face lit up a little. "Really?"

"Yeah. But I'd need someone to help me put it up."

"I could do that!" Ricky offered eagerly.

"Hmm." Flynn pretended to consider. "I guess you could. Why don't we head out to the driveway and take a look?"

Once outside, Flynn walked companionably with Ricky, waiting to see his reaction.

Ricky stopped suddenly, his eyes growing wide and round. "Wow!"

"You like it?"

"It's swell!" Then he turned to Flynn, his six-year-old eyes far too wise. "You don't need my help."

"Sure do. The pole's set. But I need help hanging the hoop."

Ricky brightened as Flynn took the ladder from the tree he'd leaned it upon.

"I tacked up the backboard," Flynn explained. "But we need to center the hoop."

"Cool!" Ricky exclaimed.

Originally he'd offered to help Ricky because of the guilt he still felt over Todd. He'd never considered that the child would come to tread on his heart, as well. Yet the connection remained painful, as though each step closer picked at the wound that was his past.

But today, standing beside the young boy who looked up at him with something nearing hero worship, another barricade tore loose.

Picking Ricky up, he sat him on his shoulders. "Okay, you center the hoop."

"By myself?" Ricky asked excitedly.

"Sure. When you get it in the center, we'll mark the spot with this thick pencil."

"Okay." Screwing his face into lines of concentration, Ricky carefully centered the hoop.

Flynn handed him the carpenter's pencil and the boy made two marks as Flynn instructed him.

They turned, Ricky still on his shoulders, just as Cindy and Noah stepped out of the house. She was dressed in a gold sequinned evening gown. With her silky red hair streaming down her back, she looked like a gorgeous flame.

And Flynn felt an invisible fist to the gut.

Noah took Cindy's elbow, guiding her down the sidewalk. Again, she looked relaxed, happy. No angst, no uncertainty.

Nothing as she looked when they were together.

Glancing up, she spotted them.

Ricky waved.

Cindy lifted her arm, as well, studying Flynn and Ricky.

"See you later!" Ricky called out.

"Yeah, have a great time," Flynn managed with notably less enthusiasm.

She nodded. "Thanks. I will."

Flynn watched as she got into the car, then as Noah pulled away.

"She looks pretty, huh?" Ricky asked.

Flynn swallowed. "She sure does."

"She's nice like Mommy," Ricky added quietly.

Flynn lifted him down from his shoulders. "She is?"

"Yeah. To the triples, too," he replied, using his own version of triplets, a word he couldn't quite conquer. "I thought they were her babies at first."

"You did?"

"Uh-huh. Excepted I knew they didn't always live here."

The world through a child's clear vision,

Flynn realized. A rare and remarkable gift. "She loves them a lot," Flynn admitted aloud.

"Cindy makes us feel special," Ricky said. "Even Heather, and she hates *everybody*."

Flynn felt an unexpected smile emerge. "Is that so?"

"Yeah. She used to do mean stuff before we had Rainbow class. Our Sunday school teacher said she couldn't come back never."

But Cindy had rescued that unlovable child. He had been a fool, Flynn realized. Purposely not seeing Cindy's depth and caring, her commitment to a group of children who had no one else to be concerned for them.

The fact was that she still drew him as she had the first moment he'd seen her.

But Julia had been safer. She hadn't threatened a true hold on his heart. And Cindy had held just such a promise in her eyes. One he guessed had been like the jolt his own father had felt when meeting his mother. A love that took precedence over everything else. One he'd been fleeing since the day Todd had been killed.

Flynn stared down the now-empty street. But this time he had run straight into that phenomenal and rare love. And she'd just driven off with another man.

★ ★ ★

Nearly four weeks later, Cindy hummed softly under her breath as she checked on the waffles she was preparing for Flynn's birthday breakfast.

In the past weeks she had pumped the girls, finding out his favorite breakfast foods. She'd listed all the traditional items, knowing he would prefer them to her buckwheat pancakes or granola and berries. Between the girls, they had remembered waffles, sausages and orange juice. Cindy had purchased regular syrup, and creamy butter, as well. It wasn't that she didn't know how to prepare traditional food, she simply preferred healthy eating.

She added a freshly cut early summer rose to the tray. Covered by her finest linen, silver, crystal and dinnerware, it looked especially appealing, she decided. Seeing the light go out on the waffle iron, she placed the waffles on the plate in a matching diagonal fashion. The sausages and juice were already on the tray.

Cindy turned to the kids. "Okay, guys, do you have everything?"

"Yes," they chorused, barely able to contain their excitement.

They trooped upstairs, but Cindy paused as she reached Flynn's doorway, her nerves

252

clicking into overdrive. She'd never before entered his territory. It didn't matter that it was her house. This was still his room.

Heart pounding, she pushed open the door. From behind and around her, the kids shouted, "Happy birthday."

Flynn's sleep-tousled head popped up. He stared at them in surprise.

Then to Cindy's relief, he grinned.

Still nervous, she approached the bed, offering the tray.

Accepting it, he glanced at the contents, then up at her in amazement. "What did I do to deserve this?"

Her eyes brightened despite her anxiety. "You were born."

He smiled. "Waffles *and* sausages?"

"We told Cinny you liked 'em," Beth offered.

"And orange juice," Mandy added.

"We have another surprise," Cindy added, motioning to the kids.

They scampered out to the hall, returning quickly, carrying musical instruments. Although Ricky didn't really play one, Cindy had found a tambourine for him.

"You going to serenade me, as well?" Flynn asked in pleased surprise.

Cindy picked up her own mandolin that Ricky had fetched from the hall. On her signal, they began to play. Flynn continued smiling, but his eyes widened when the girls' sweet voices added the words "I'm so glad you're my daddy."

Even Ricky sang along, and Cindy saw Flynn's jaw work.

When the song ended, Flynn set the tray on one side of the bed, reaching out to hug his daughters and Ricky. His voice when he spoke was gruff. "Thank you. That was the best birthday present I ever got."

"We boughted more stuff for you!" Beth revealed.

"And wrapped it all up," Mandy added.

Alice smiled sweetly. "It's surprises."

Flynn lifted his eyes, meeting Cindy's. "I don't think I need any more surprises. This was the best."

And her heart weakened, as the hold he held on it strengthened. Pulling her gaze from his, she glanced down at the children. "Okay, you want to go get the presents?"

They clapped and squealed in agreement, scampering away.

Flynn looked at the carefully prepared tray. "How did you possibly know all my favorites?"

Despite the tug-of-war in her heart, she grinned. "Some little fairies told me. You

have to be careful. These little fairies are en-
cyclopedias of information."

He returned her grin. "Even better than
the Internet."

Their gazes met and lingered, the grins
giving way to something else.

"Thank you," Flynn told her quietly.

It seemed to Cindy that the words reso-
nated beyond what they appeared on the
surface. She knew her own did. "You're
welcome."

"Look, Daddy!" Beth hollered, skidding
into the room. "Presents!" She dumped her
own awkwardly wrapped gift on his bed.

The other children followed, piling presents on the bed.

Flynn picked up Beth's, using great care
to open the clumsily assembled package. He
held up a T-shirt emblazoned with a picture
of Donald Duck.

"I picked it!" Beth exclaimed.

Amused, Flynn lifted his gaze to meet
Cindy's. "Really?"

"She had a hard time choosing between
that one and Winnie the Pooh," Cindy explained, unable to hide her own smile.

Flynn hugged his daughter. "Well, this is
the one I would have picked, too. It's perfect. Thank you, Beth."

Pleased, Beth grinned as Flynn opened

the next one, which was from Alice.

"Oh, this is great," he replied, holding up a huge chocolate bar.

"You like it?" Alice asked.

He hugged her, as well. "It's almost as sweet as you."

"Mine now," Mandy demanded.

Obliging, Flynn unwrapped two coloring books and a huge box of crayons. He glanced between Mandy and Cindy, clearly trying not to sound either puzzled or amused. "Wow."

"We can color together," Mandy told him, beaming at the prospect.

"So we can." A third hug was dispensed. "What a great idea."

Ricky shyly pushed forward his present next.

"I'm getting pretty overwhelmed," Flynn admitted.

He was, Cindy realized.

Flynn unwrapped the present, revealing a baseball cap.

"It's got the Rangers on it," Ricky explained. "Your favorite."

Flynn's throat worked. "You're right. They are my favorites. Thanks." More awkwardly this time, Flynn offered Ricky a hug, as well.

Cindy's own emotions tumbled as she

watched them, thinking how perfect they looked together.

"Yours now!" Beth told her.

"Oh, yes." Cindy handed him a small, neatly wrapped box.

His gaze touched hers. Then he opened the gift, unfolding the tissue that was tucked inside, then lifting up the present. He held up a framed portrait of the triplets. They were wearing dresses Flynn had chosen for them, a triple play of perfection.

"How?" he asked in wonder. "When?"

"I have my ways," Cindy replied. "We snuck off when you weren't looking."

"It's wonderful," Flynn said softly. "Really wonderful."

"There's something else in the box," she told him.

He dug beneath another layer of tissue, uncovering a second framed picture. Again his throat worked as he turned it around to show the others the picture of a shyly smiling Ricky.

The girls clapped and Ricky stubbed the toe of his tennis shoe into the thick rug, his pleasure overshadowing his timidity.

"You really are a magician," Flynn said finally.

And his hold on her heart gripped even tighter.

Chapter Fifteen

†

"What are you guys doing here?" Flynn asked, looking up from his work to the crowd standing in his doorway.

Cindy touched the glass block wall that separated Flynn's office from a large working area, one that had half walls of the same material to give each employee a degree of privacy. "This place looks great! Michael did a wonderful job on the remodeling. Looks kind of retro.

"To answer your question — I've got a scheduling conflict," she explained ruefully. "Katherine's booked solid and I've called everyone else I know. I can't find a sitter, so . . ."

Flynn glanced down at his daughters' expectant faces. "Oh, sure. I'll find something to keep them busy."

Ricky held up a canvas tote bag. "We brought markers and Play-Doh and blocks."

Cindy raised up a second bag. "And snacks and juice."

Flynn wriggled his brows at the children. "I don't know. We might just get crazy, bust out of here and get some pizza."

But Cindy only grinned. "Great. Give them plenty of sugar, too, because you'll be in charge of naptime, as well."

"You must have a long date planned," Flynn probed in what he hoped was a casual voice.

"Actually, it's a photo session. Can you believe it? Noah says someone caught our act, and he actually thinks we can promote the band."

Flynn caught only one word at first — *Noah*. So that's who she'd ditched the children for. Then he shook his head. "What did you say?"

"I know. It doesn't seem possible. But apparently some people from Dallas were at our last gig and really liked the sound. Personally, I don't want the travel involved in band commitments that far away, but I don't mind posing for the publicity pictures. Noah can always replace me if he decides to get that cosmopolitan."

"Band?" Flynn managed to spit out.

She cocked her head, drawing her brows together in a puzzled manner. "You know, the one Noah and I play in. The one that came to the girls' party."

"You weren't in the band that day," he replied, still not grasping her explanation.

Cindy looked faintly exasperated. "No, I was a little busy with the party and being the clown. Why?"

Flynn cleared his throat. "How often do you play in this band?"

She shrugged. "I never kept track of exactly how often. But you've seen me dressed in costume when Noah picks me up for a performance. It's not like Rosewood has enough proms, parties and anniversaries to keep us busy every day. To be truthful, since you and the girls moved here, I've cut back on my participation a lot. Noah's real understanding about it." She laughed. "He only pleads when he can't find a backup player and singer."

"Doesn't that intrude on your relationship?" Flynn asked, pushing the envy from his voice with great effort.

She blinked. "Our friendship's fine. As I said, Noah's very understanding. I guess it comes from being a doctor. He has to back out on so many social commitments because of emergencies that it's hard for him to even find time to date. I think that's why he doesn't have a girlfriend."

Buzzers and whistles clamored so loudly in Flynn's head, he wondered if he'd imagined her reply. "He doesn't have a girlfriend?"

Expression sad, Cindy shook her head. "No. And I think he's lonely even though he's so busy. You know what I mean?"

Flynn knew exactly what she meant. The longing for that one special person to be in your arms, the need for a true partner. The feeling maybe it would never be possible. At least . . . not until now.

"Flynn?" Cindy asked, her eyes puzzled again.

"Right. Yeah, I do know what you mean. So, what are you doing after the photo shoot?"

She shrugged. "Nothing. We don't have a gig tonight."

"But you have to dress up for the pictures?"

She rolled her eyes. "Full tilt. That's why my dress is in the car. I'd look a little ridiculous driving around in the middle of the day dressed in an evening gown."

Flynn studied her face, the sparkle in her eyes. "Does seem like a shame to get all dressed up, then have nowhere to go. Do you think we can find a place here in Rosewood to do it justice? *If* I can locate a baby-sitter."

Clearly taken aback, she stuttered at first. "We-well I guess so. There's a little Italian restaurant with a dance floor that's only a little bigger than a half dollar, but it's dressy for Rosewood."

"Then it's a date?"

She flushed, not a gentle warming, but a wave of red. "A date?"

"You know that thing where two people go out —" he lowered his voice to a mock whisper "— *without* the kids."

Cindy looked at the kids' intrigued faces, then back to Flynn. "Uh, okay. Sure."

"Don't get too carried away with your enthusiasm."

She backed out of the doorway. "No, of course not." She bumped into a chair, then muttered, "Sorry."

Flynn's brows rose and even the children studied her curiously.

"I'd better be going," Cindy told him fervently.

"I'll see you tonight."

"Tonight," she agreed, bumping into another chair, muttering a second apology to the inanimate object.

Flynn watched as she left, marveling at how even her haste was animated.

Beth reached up, tugging on his hand. "What do we do now?"

What indeed?

Nervously Cindy checked her hair, which

she'd partially swept up. The insistent curl in its texture escaped to frame her face. Hair okay, she decided, turning to look in the cheval mirror, checking her dress again.

It was ridiculous. She hadn't primped this much for the stupid photo shoot. Picking up the petite gold purse that matched her dress, she reluctantly headed downstairs.

It's just dinner. Dinner with the man you've been in love with for years. Put the brakes on, she chastised herself. He's the man you can't even consider sharing a future with.

Halfway down the stairs, she caught sight of Flynn, pacing in the foyer. She had seen him dressed in suits before, but the one he'd chosen for tonight was of a European cut, adding another layer of sophistication.

She guessed all the female heads in the small restaurant would positively crane in his direction. Willing her nerves to settle, she traveled down the last few steps.

Hearing her, Flynn spun around, then stopped as quickly. "I was right. You do look like a flame."

Pleased, embarrassed, nearly thrilled, Cindy ducked her head. "Flatterer."

He took a few steps closer. "Just telling the truth."

The nerves in her stomach were rattling

her brains. "Well, should we go?"

He picked up a solitary rose from the hall table and extended the flower.

"It's nearly gold," she marveled, seeing that its deep yellow petals almost matched the dress.

"I was hoping you'd wear the gold. It suits you."

She bit her bottom lip. "A flame that flickers?"

"And warms everyone in its proximity."

Beyond flattered and touched, she could merely stare.

But Flynn took her elbow, escorting her to the door.

Once inside the car, she stole a look at him. "Tell me how you convinced Michael to watch the kids tonight."

Flynn's expression grew rueful. "I promised to play on their softball team the rest of the summer."

"Oh, I see. True blackmail."

Flynn chuckled. "I thought it was worth the sacrifice."

Cindy averted her head, staring out the window. "How's the construction coming on your house?"

"It's close to being finished. I checked the site today."

"That's good," she replied, thinking it

wouldn't be long now. Flynn would move his daughters to their new home and her relationship with them would never be quite the same.

It didn't take long to reach the restaurant. Despite the fact that it was Rosewood's most elegant restaurant, Flynn and Cindy's attire still drew glances.

"Do you suppose they'll believe we just came from the prom?" Flynn whispered.

She grinned. "I don't think I can pass for eighteen even in my wildest dreams."

He leaned forward, barely touching one of the runaway curls that brushed her cheek. "I don't know. I think I'd buy it."

"Your table's ready," the hostess announced.

Shaken, Cindy was grateful for the reprieve.

Once their order was taken, Flynn glanced at the small quartet that provided the background music. "Would you like to dance?"

That sounded entirely too dangerous. "Oh, I don't think so. With these fancy outfits we'd probably be awfully conspicuous."

Flynn leaned back in his chair. "You know, Cindy, you never told me why you really moved to Rosewood. If you were running to someone . . . or away from someone."

And this was even more dangerous. "Who cares if they think we look like escapees from our senior, senior prom?" She stood abruptly. "So, you still want to dance?"

He stood, as well, extending his hand.

Accepting it, Cindy felt the connection the moment her hand touched his. But when he took her in his arms, her heart cratered. She'd dreamed of this moment, longed for it, despaired of it ever happening.

But in her dreams, he wasn't meant to be kept at arm's length. Still, she allowed him to lead her around the dance floor, to feel for this solitary moment how it would be to spend all time with him.

She felt the whisper of his breath on her cheek, the texture of his hair, the strength of his hands and arms, the structure of his tall frame. And for that moment, she let her imagination wander, to envision a future with him.

The music slowed to a halt, its progression matching her hopes. She declined a second dance, instead suggesting they order.

"Is something wrong?" Flynn asked when she continued to be unusually quiet.

She shook her head. "Just thinking."

"Do you want to share your thoughts?"

Cindy searched his eyes, seeing the sincerity, the puzzlement. And for another moment she didn't want to ruin this exceptional evening. She lifted her glass. "Why don't we just enjoy our dinner?"

His expression wavered, then he nodded.

The food came, warm and fragrant. They tasted the homemade linguini, the sauce pungent with fresh tomatoes and basil. Yet, there was more food than conversation.

"It's not quite the same as on the Riverwalk," Flynn mused.

Her gaze met his, that remembered moment stretching between them, begging to be felt again.

"No," she agreed at last. "That was unique . . . a rare time."

After declining dessert, Flynn suggested they walk along Main Street, a leftover from the previous century with its old false-fronted buildings.

The summer breeze teased the branches of the tall, ancient trees that lined the street, their branches stretching out to meet in the middle of the road. During the day they provided shady relief; at night they seemed to shelter.

"It's a beautiful evening," Cindy remarked, pulling her antique silk shawl closer.

Flynn stopped, turning to her. "Not as

beautiful as you." He leaned toward her.

For one brief and dazzling moment she considered letting herself fall into the kiss he offered . . . into all the romantic fantasies she'd ever had of this moment.

But the pleasure of the kiss would also be like a bruise to her soul. Knowing that, she pulled back, brushing him away. "Please . . . don't."

He stared at her. "Are you telling me I've misread the signals? That there wasn't something between us that evening in San Antonio? That there isn't something between us now?"

She shook her head, starting to turn away.

But he caught her elbow. "Then why are you rejecting me?"

"Let's stop now," she pleaded, knowing his three children would always remain a connection between them, one that might not take the damage of the truth.

"Why?" Flynn demanded. "Why should I stop?"

"Don't do this," she begged again.

"Look at me, Cindy. Tell me you aren't feeling like I do. That you don't want to take our relationship to this next step."

Her lips trembled with the force of holding in the truth. "I can't tell you those things because they aren't true." She lifted her gaze, willing her heart to settle long enough to spit out what she must. "But it's not that easy."

"Why not?" he demanded.

She swallowed. "I cannot love a man who doesn't share my faith."

"Do you want me to lie?" he asked bluntly.

Her heart fractured with pain. "That would only be worse. I can't live a falsehood, and I can't accept anything less than a man of equal beliefs. I'm sorry, Flynn."

"And that's it?" he asked in disbelief.

She hesitated, remembering her recent prayers for guidance. "Perhaps it's not impossible, if you're willing to try."

He scowled. "In what way?"

She ducked her head, afraid to see the anger she knew was coming. "Maybe by revisiting the past."

His snort conveyed anger and more. "That's not a trip I ever want to take again."

Knowing his reaction was born of pain, she caught his hand, leading him to a bench that curved around a large oak tree in the sidewalk. "I know this is hard for you, Flynn." She met his eyes, willing him to understand. "We've both suffered loss. It hurts, even when you've pushed it to the back of your mind. But I've been thinking a lot about what you told me . . . about your past."

He started to pull his hand away, but Cindy held it that much more firmly.

"Flynn, have you ever considered that perhaps your mother took her life because she was consumed with guilt over Todd?" Cindy gentled her voice even further. "Maybe she was afraid that she would cause a similar fate for you. Perhaps it was less of an abandonment, rather a sacrifice." Cindy tightened her grasp on his hand. "Oh, Flynn think how anguished she must have been, the fact that she couldn't have been thinking clearly, rather responding to the love she felt for her sons."

He was quiet, absently rubbing his thumb over her fingers. "She just left. She let Todd get killed, then she died."

"From a nine-year-old perspective," Cindy reminded him quietly. "You're a parent, now. Imagine how you would feel if your negligence cost the life of one of your daughters. Do you suppose you'd be thinking straight? Making responsible decisions?"

"She never was responsible," Flynn replied, the old bitterness seeping out, bit by bit. He lifted his head, meeting Cindy's eyes. "That's why I chose Julia, you know.

She was nothing like my mother. I was sure she'd be stable, secure, always there."

"And even that collapsed when she died," Cindy replied, clamping down on her own pain. Flynn *had* chosen the right sister. Julia was everything he needed, everything she wasn't. Yet, Cindy knew she couldn't put her own feelings ahead of his crisis of faith. "Flynn, I think the pain you feel from losing your brother . . . your entire family will always haunt you. I'm no Pollyanna. I know the past can't just be erased. But you can put what happened into perspective."

"I don't think that's possible," he replied dully.

"There's one way . . . Forgive your mother."

Anguished, Flynn stared at her. "How can I possibly forgive her?"

Cindy swallowed, knowing how difficult the next words would be for him to hear. "By reconnecting with the Lord."

"That's impossible!" he railed, pulling away from her. "You don't know what you're asking!"

"I've had an equal share of loss, Flynn. Both my parents, my only sister. But my bond with the Lord is even stronger than ever before."

"How can I hope to forgive? To reconstruct a faith lost in childhood?"

"Through prayer." Cindy met his eyes, her own bright with unshed tears. "Just a few simple words . . . ones from your soul."

But Flynn only stared ahead.

Cindy didn't know if he'd even heard her, if the words had simply washed over him like the fingers of moonlight stabbing through the overhanging branches. Or if he'd already cast them aside.

Chapter Sixteen

†

Flynn accepted the baseball glove, tucking it into his gym bag. He and Michael Carlson were the last ones left on the practice field.

"Something wrong?" Michael asked quietly.

Distracted, Flynn cleared his thoughts, then shook his head. "Not really."

"That was said with a distinct lack of conviction," Michael noted.

Shrugging, Flynn zipped up the bag. "Just a lot on my mind."

"Want to talk about it?"

For several long moments, Flynn contemplated the problem, the issue of sharing it. "I doubt it's something you can help with."

"Try me."

So Flynn explained his recent discussion with Cindy, briefly outlining why he'd lost his faith initially.

But the other man surprised him. Michael looked neither shocked nor displeased. And he didn't directly address the faith issue. "Do you still think Cindy's as flighty as your mother was?"

"No. I think I've finally taken off my blinders. Cindy . . ." Flynn chuckled. "Well, you know how she is. You pointed it out yourself." Flynn's quiet laugh turned into a contemplative sigh. "But I couldn't see it then — my past was getting in the way. I've never known anyone like her before. She's caring, compassionate. She has so much energy, it's like being around a constant whirlwind, yet at the same time . . ." Flynn glanced up sheepishly. "Guess it's my turn for the *Oprah* segment."

But Michael only shook his head. "Nah. You've just gotten tangled up with a wildcat. And I mean that only in a good way."

"Yeah," Flynn agreed. "The rare combination of brains, personality, heart and spunk."

Michael studied him. "So, are you ready to try what she's asked?"

"I'm not so sure."

"That's how I felt," Michael confided.

"You?"

Michael grinned. "Being married to a minister doesn't make me a saint."

Flynn raised his eyebrows.

"Before I met Katherine, my wife, Ruth, died. When she got sick I prayed, my family prayed, the whole congregation prayed. But she still died. And I couldn't get past the fact that the Lord had let that happen. Ruth was a good person, fair, kind, always looking out for everyone else. I just assumed that meant He was looking out for her. And nothing anybody said or did could change how I felt."

"But you go to church now."

Michael smiled. "It's more than attendance for me. I've regained my faith, but it wasn't easy. The journey back was even more painful than losing Ruth. If it weren't for Katherine, I'd still be stumbling in the dark." He shrugged. "Since I'm back on the right path, everything is right with my life. I have a beautiful wife, a new son, my other children are happy." Michael met Flynn's eyes. "And that wouldn't have happened otherwise."

"You're so sure?"

"I don't have a single doubt."

Flynn nodded. "Thanks."

"Now you just have one more talk."

"With who?"

Michael looked at him pointedly.

"Oh, the prayer thing."

"Yeah. I'll clear out." Michael started to turn away, then glanced back. "You won't regret it, Flynn. I'm sure of it."

Flynn watched as Michael walked away,

the field suddenly empty. The hottest part of the day was past, the sun past the day's prime. The air was still; not even the barest breeze stirred the dry grass or the dusty pitcher's mound.

It was rare for him to be this alone, Flynn realized. There was something oddly revealing about the solitude. It was more difficult to make excuses . . . to hang on to anger from a past era.

Tilting his head backward, Flynn studied the graying sky. And he wondered. Could Cindy and Flynn be right? Was it only a matter of words?

For an interminable time, Flynn considered and rejected a thousand beginnings. He started, stopped, then started again. Finally the prayer stumbled out . . . fumbling, unpoetic words. But they were from his heart. Briefly he closed his eyes, wondering if he spoke to an empty field, an empty sky.

Then a warmth he hadn't known since childhood filled his heart. Again Flynn closed his eyes, gripped by the power of this new truth.

And suddenly the field was no longer empty, the shadows no longer growing. Flynn lifted his head, staring into the heavens. One thought penetrated the wonder. He had to tell Cindy how he felt about her. How he really felt about her.

Flynn wanted this incredible woman in his life. The woman who had set him free. And who, he hoped, would share his love.

The evening sky was settling stars in formation before Flynn reached the house. From the study windows, Cindy watched for him, knowing softball practice should have ended some time before. It didn't seem much could happen to him in a small place like Rosewood, yet she couldn't help worrying.

She'd put the girls to bed, but Ricky was still up, waiting for Flynn. As much as she was growing to love the child, it was Flynn that filled the loneliness in Ricky's life, the one he turned to.

Hearing the front door open, Ricky scooted through the kitchen and into the foyer. Cindy followed more slowly, watching as Flynn scooped up the boy, hugging him. Then he set him back on the floor, ruffling his hair, keeping one hand on his shoulder.

Her gaze met Flynn's. Something about him was different. She couldn't place it, yet she was certain. "I saved you some dinner."

"I don't suppose it's that great veggie lasagna?"

She stared at him in surprise. "Do you really like it?"

"Sure. It's great. Not as good as your crab puffs, but still great."

Cindy considered checking his I.D. Was this really Flynn Mallory? "Well, actually I did make lasagna."

Flynn glanced down at Ricky. "Have you eaten?"

"Uh-huh. But I could eat more," he offered hopefully.

Flynn glanced at Cindy. "Do you mind?"

She shook her head, still wondering at his easy manner. "No, it's fine." Then she glanced down at Ricky. "A small piece for you?"

"Okay. Does this mean we can have more brownies, too?"

Cindy smiled tolerantly. "Why not?"

But it didn't take long for Ricky to start tiring. Soon his eyelids were drooping.

Flynn glanced at Cindy. "Maybe the guys ought to head upstairs."

"I'm not tired," Ricky protested, fighting a yawn.

" 'Course not." Flynn pretended to yawn, stretching his long arms upward. "But I am. Want to keep me company?"

Ricky yawned again. "Okay."

Cindy watched them leave, the tall man,

the very small child. It shouldn't affect her so, she knew. But it was a tender picture.

She rinsed the plates and stacked them in the dishwasher. Remembering that Flynn had liked her limeade, she pulled out some limes, squeezing them into a pale pink, Depression glass pitcher. Once it was ready, she hung maraschino cherries from matching pink glasses.

Flynn entered the kitchen as she was arranging the tray.

"I thought we could take this outside," she offered as he crossed the room to stand beside her. Close beside her.

She started to lift the tray, but Flynn took it from her, carrying it out the open French doors. Once she was seated, he put the tray on the table then pulled up a chair right next to hers.

Cindy kept sneaking glances at him, wondering what was up with him. "How'd practice go?"

He shrugged. "I doubt we're ready for the major leagues, but it's coming together."

"Mmm." She let a few moments pass. "So, nothing out of the ordinary?"

He met her gaze. "Such as?"

She shrugged away the question. "Limeade? It's the one I make with —"

"Maraschino cherries." His gaze met hers. "I know."

Cindy licked her lips nervously. "Of course you do."

The limeade was just sweet enough, the night just quiet enough . . . the tension between them, however, rising higher than the new moon.

"Cindy?"

She jumped, sloshing the limeade. "Yes?"

"There's something we didn't talk about the other night."

"Oh?"

"About how we felt when we met."

She swallowed. "That was a long time ago."

"And we were very different people then."

Her head jerked up. "You think so?"

"Don't you?"

She stared at him hopelessly. "But you haven't noticed that I've changed, that —"

He leaned even closer. Reaching out he took her hand. "Have I waited too long?"

Pain sweltered, its heat dissolving her hope. Now she recognized the new emotion in Flynn's demeanor and expression. He was confusing loneliness for something more. A man accustomed to being married, now adrift on his own. She'd known men and women like him before — people who could not emotionally bear to be on their own, even though they were unrelentingly self-sufficient. And soon he would be on his own — his new house lacked only finishing touches.

But companionship wasn't enough for her. It was a great and true love, or nothing. "It's not a matter of time."

Flynn's expression dimmed, his eyes narrowing. "What then?"

She battled tears and temptation. "I can't be a substitute for Julia."

"I didn't say I wanted that!"

"No. But I've become a comfortable habit. Caring for the girls, doing the things Julia always did, trying to fill the place in your lives that she left."

"Comfortable?" he questioned incredulously. "That's how you think I feel about you?"

But Cindy had tussled with this question far longer than he had. "Let's be honest, Flynn. When we met, you chose Julia, not me. And fundamentally I *am* still that person. Wiser, more mature, more compassionate, but I'm still not demure and refined. I'm noisy, bullheaded and opinionated." She clutched the arm of the wicker chair for support. "And I wouldn't change myself to suit you if I could."

"I haven't asked you to change," he protested.

Sadly she met his gaze. "No, but it's what you would want. I can never be like Julia." She swallowed again. "Let's face it. You've been running from a woman like me since the day you lost your brother. That's why you chose Julia, why you need someone like her. We may be sisters, but as you've pointed out, we're so different we could have been conceived on separate planets."

"Cindy, you're not listening to me. I know who you are . . . who I want."

She gazed at his sincere face, wishing she could believe him, wishing that for once her heart would overrule her head. But it wasn't to be. She couldn't open herself to more hurt, knowing the ultimate outcome, the disappointment he would feel when he realized how very little she was like her sister.

More important, Cindy couldn't give her love to a man of unequal yoke. "That's just it. You don't know me." She bit down on her lip to stop its trembling. "And neither one of us needs the disappointment."

Flynn searched her expression. "You really believe I just want a substitute?"

Cindy thought of all the lonely nights, the longing for a husband and family of her own, the love she'd hidden for years. Despite that, she couldn't be second best. And so she withdrew her hand from his. Despite the ebony night, she could see the confused disbelief in his eyes.

And knew it matched her own.

Chapter Seventeen

†

Persistence had always paid off for Flynn. When he'd worked three jobs to put himself through college, when he had convinced a bank to loan him the seed money for his first business, when he'd taken that company from a struggling one-man outfit to a premier international insurance firm.

But Cindy was a tougher nut to crack than any of those. And so Flynn decided he had to woo her. As romantically and creatively as ever was done.

For nearly three weeks he had tried chocolates, flowers, perfume, romantic picnics, evening strolls. And one thing was certain.

He hadn't changed her mind at all. It was as though she tolerated the gestures, but didn't take them too seriously, still believing he saw her only in Julia's shadow. She even considered his recent church attendance to be nothing more than a show for her benefit.

It would take more, he realized. Not simple, traditional courting methods. It had to be something that blew her socks off.

And he could think of only one possible choice.

He glanced over at Cindy, uncomfortably scrunched close to the car door on her side. As far away from him as possible.

He withheld a sigh, turning into the recently completed driveway. "Here we are."

Her face was unreadable as she looked up at his new house. "So we are."

Before she could step from the car on her own, he was beside her door, opening it.

Her gaze encompassed the large, modern structure. "It really is lovely."

"Nothing like your house, though."

Cindy stared at the entrance again, a wisp of sadness coloring her expression. "No. Not at all."

"Let's go inside."

She nodded, allowing him to guide her up the walk.

They passed through the arched courtyard that was a mix between a classic Italian style with Tuscan columns and Mediterranean tile and a more casual atrium. It had been designed to be inviting, much like the wraparound porch was at Cindy's house. But at the same time, it offered a bit of privacy.

Once inside, surveying the interior, Flynn tried to see the house through her eyes, ones so very different than his own. He pointed to the unusual striped arches over the doorways in the entry hall. "Dark Texas Pecos sandstone," he explained. "The lighter stone is granite."

"I like it," she responded quietly, the sadness in her face making its way into her voice. "It's different, and I always appreciate using native materials."

"I like contemporary, but I'm not crazy about living in a barren box." He pointed toward the tall windows in the next room. "There's a loggia in the back that I want to be cozy, like your terrace."

Flynn led her deeper into the house.

"The design is good," she commented as they stepped into the great room that seemed all windows and white walls. "With warm decorating, it won't be sterile."

"Glad you brought that up."

She lifted her gaze. "Oh?"

Flynn felt himself falling into that gaze, wishing he could simply offer the shelter of his embrace, that she would believe how much he valued her. "Well, actually, I want to ask you a huge favor."

"What is it?"

"I'd like you to decorate the house."

Clearly stunned, she stared at him. "What did you say?"

He smiled, pleased to see the sadness chased away by surprise. "I think you heard me. I'd like you to decorate the house."

She studied his expression. "I don't get it. My style couldn't be more different than yours."

"Please?"

Swallowing, she turned again to look at the clean lines of the room. "So, what do you have in mind?"

"Put your stamp on it, your distinctive sense of style."

Cindy frowned. "Why mine?"

He shrugged. "Could we call it one last gift in a long list of things you've done for me, the girls?"

Cindy clasped her hands together, the nervous gesture as betraying as the dark pain she tried to hide. "Why don't I copy what Julia chose for your home in Houston? I remember it pretty well."

"No. It wouldn't suit you. I'm not looking for a substitute for Julia. Not in my house. Not in my life. Just as I don't want you to change yourself, to imitate her. You're no substitute, Cindy. It's your style I want in my house."

Her face filled with wonder and disbelief. "But . . . what if you hate it? What if —"

"What if you let me decide the things I like and want?"

A month later Cindy was still mulling over his words. She couldn't help wondering exactly what Flynn had meant by them. They'd already resolved that she would never be a substitute for Julia. And yet, no amount of arguing would convince him that she shouldn't be the one decorating his new house. When they were at the final impasse, he'd told her flatly that he and the girls would stay at her house until she agreed.

Although part of her would like nothing better, Cindy knew she couldn't take the daily torture of having Flynn in her house much longer, knowing they had no future.

So she'd thrown herself into the project, taking time out only for her Rainbow class which the triplets attended and, of course, the triplets themselves. The rest of her hours were spent studying colors, textures, fabrics and furniture. She told herself that she was spending the time as part of her on-going endeavor to help the girls. But in reality, she needed the distance from Flynn, from the feelings she couldn't control. Luckily Noah found a temporary replacement for her in the band so that wasn't a distraction.

Thinking surely Flynn would want to ship

at least some of his belongings to the new house, she'd pressed him again. But Flynn was unyielding. He had already arranged for an estate agency to auction everything in storage, which should bring in an amount at least equal to his new decorating budget.

When Cindy heard that, she'd gulped in apprehension. What if he didn't like what she chose? What would he replace it with?

Flynn showed no concern whatsoever.

Which made Cindy that much more nervous.

His only specific request was that she decorate the guest room in a style suitable for a young boy, for Ricky when he visited, Flynn explained.

Although she urged Flynn to inspect the house as she chose first the paint colors, then rugs for the wood and tile floors, he declined. Nor would he accompany her to furniture stores or galleries in either Rosewood or Houston, insisting he wanted the house to have her exclusive style.

So the first week she picked out the colors and hired painters. Then she shopped. It was a challenge. She wanted the house to be masculine, yet comfortable for the girls. And, some of her own whimsy and playfulness also incorporated itself in the decorating. She was glad to be putting her own stamp on the house, knowing a small part of her would remain with him.

It was a mixed feeling, the joy of doing something special for the man she loved, tempered by the sadness of knowing how much she would miss Flynn and the girls. And as the long summer days eventually shortened, so did her hope.

Three weeks later, Cindy was ready to show Flynn the completed project. They'd spent very little time together since she'd started working on the house. When Flynn came home from the office, she left him with the children, spending each evening at the new house.

Now, despite the time she'd poured into the work, she was anxious about his reaction.

Glancing over at him, she swallowed. It was a place for play, for living, for love. She was a mass of nerves as they stepped out of his car. "You know I'm a collector at heart, but I also have very eclectic tastes."

"Hmm," he agreed noncommittally.

Entering the walled courtyard, they were immediately shaded and surrounded by varying-sized plants she had nestled into the cool space. She'd also added a nineteenth-century fountain that spilled a calming stream of water near the flora. The now-serene alcove appeared almost European, with its now seemingly aged charm.

"I hope you like plants," she continued, still feeling like a tour guide instructing a reluctant tourist.

"Yes."

Cindy wondered at the brief reply as she used the key he'd given her to unlock the front door. She handed him the key, knowing she wouldn't need it again.

They stepped into the entry hall, which she'd had painted in a warm terra-cotta wash that highlighted the beautiful stonework above the doorways. A simple table in the center of the hall held a sleek vase filled with yellow flowers.

"I know guys don't usually have flowers," she explained anxiously. "But they give such life to a house."

"I like it," he remarked, strolling on to the great room.

It took her a moment to absorb that. Then realizing he was walking forward, she scurried to catch up. Uneasily she watched for his reaction to the main living area. She'd had the walls painted a warm, honey yellow that seemed to glow, almost at one with the light flowing in the ceiling-to-floor windows. A thick, comfortable rug anchored the room.

She had interspersed leather club chairs with a warm fabric sofa. The antique armoire that held the television and VCR was a pleasant contrast to the sleek furniture.

"I was going for warm but modern," she explained earnestly. "For you and three growing, constantly changing girls."

Flynn didn't say anything, instead turning slowly in the space.

"And upstairs," she continued nervously. "Even though you gave the girls a three-room suite, I thought each room should have its own character, so although the colors harmonize, each one's different. Is that okay?"

He didn't answer, still looking around the great room.

"Flynn?"

Finally he turned to her. "No, Cindy, it's not okay."

He reached for her hand, turning it palm up, then dropping the key into her grasp.

Disappointment rushed through her. He really did hate it.

"It's far more than okay." His gaze traveled over the soft lamps, the incredible artwork. "It's like you. Singularly unique. One of a kind. Which is why I love you."

Cindy desperately wanted to believe his

words, but the fragments of logic she still possessed overruled her heart. "I can't be a stand-in for Julia. I have to be loved for myself, not because I helped you or the girls." Her words stumbled. "It has to be all or nothing."

"Then let's choose all."

Cindy's eyes pleaded with him. "You had your true love. And I deserve that, as well."

Flynn pulled her an inch closer. "Don't you see that I do? How incredibly unique and wonderful you are?"

Afraid to believe, she shook her head.

His eyes darkened to beyond ebony. "I never knew before what real love was. You're right. I've been hiding from it all my life. But I know now. And it's because you're an original."

Cindy swallowed, wishing . . . wondering.

"I've grown to know the value of a meteor that streaks through life." He reached out, gently touching her vibrant tresses. "I want a woman with red hair and a personality to match."

"But . . . I'm so different."

His eyes warmed in a way she'd never seen before. "Exactly. Don't you understand? I don't want to curtail your enthusiasm, I want to embrace it. I want to squeeze the last drop of goodness from every day like you do." He tucked back a lock of her wildly curling hair. "With you."

Her lips trembled. "Oh, Flynn . . ."

"Will you marry me, Cindy? In your church? The one I've come to believe in again?"

Cindy's eyes filled and she couldn't control the quivering of her lips. "I must be dreaming, or you are. . . ."

"No, for the first time in a long time I know exactly where I am, where I want to be, who I want to be with."

"Are you sure, Flynn? About your faith? About me?"

He nodded. "You were right. I hadn't prayed since I was nine, so I was pretty rusty. But He didn't seem to mind." Flynn's hands rested on her shoulders. "And I'm just as sure about you. My life will never be the same without you. You're the light that I've needed forever, that I never believed existed. The one I ran away from the day I met you."

"And you're sure you still don't want to run away?"

"I want to run toward you, Cindy, toward a future brighter than I ever guessed was possible."

Cindy's eyes closed briefly in a prayer of thanksgiving, in happiness greater than she'd ever known.

And when he pulled her into his arms, she knew it was no dream, but a reality hoped for . . . and prayed for.

His lips were gentle as they touched hers. Their joy was as bright as the persistent beams of the late-afternoon sun.

"I love you," she said with wonder, never having believed the words could be uttered aloud to him.

He reached for her hand, his fingers strong, his heart gentle. "Then I believe this is mine."

Epilogue

†

Sixteen months later

Three matching faces lined up in front of the nursery at Rosewood Memorial Hospital.

"Are you sure ours will be that little?" Beth asked.

Ricky nodded. "Sure, they're always little when they're born." Formally adopted by Cindy and Flynn, he had stepped naturally into the role of older brother, and the triplets both revered and loved him to pieces.

"Will it go live in the children's house?" Mandy asked, referring to Cindy's old Victorian home that Cindy had donated for a children's shelter.

" 'Course not. That's why they had that other bedroom built on the house." Ricky glanced up, seeing the nurse's reproving expression. The woman had agreed to watch them until an adult arrived, but she was all business. "We better go sit down."

"Yeah," Beth agreed, second in command to Ricky as the most assertive triplet.

"Daddy said we had to be quiet or we couldn't stay."

"Miss Katherine's supposed to be here," Mandy fretted, anxious without her father or Cindy in sight.

"She's on her way," Ricky explained for the dozenth time. "The baby wasn't supposed to come till next week. Dad said she's driving here from Houston. And Miss Donna's sick so she couldn't come." Ricky's face screwed into a frown, peering toward the labor and delivery rooms. "I wonder what they're doing in there. We've been here *forever.*"

Actually it was barely a few hours. But down the hall, Flynn was wondering about many things, as well.

How he'd come to have such an incredible wife, how she'd changed his life in such a short time. He remembered their simple but beautiful wedding. The triplets had all been flower girls, Ricky the ring bearer. Michael had been pleased to be his best man and Katherine, as matron of honor, had beamed the entire time. But no one had radiated like his Cindy. *His* Cindy.

Together they were a family in the truest sense, with Ricky and the girls. Flynn had never before felt such a complete sense of belonging as he did in the fellowship of their church. He could depend on the Lord, as well as his many trusted friends.

It was a funny thing, under Cindy's tutelage he'd learned that love was the one thing that increased as you gave it away. The more love he gave to others, the fuller his life became.

Cindy's hand squeezed Flynn's more tightly, and he smoothed the hair back from her forehead. "He's beautiful, isn't he?" she asked in a soft voice.

"Almost as beautiful as his mother," Flynn replied, believing no woman could ever compare to his wife.

A few tears spilled on to her cheeks.

"Tears now?" he asked in surprise.

She nodded tremulously. "You bet."

He smiled, delighted as always by her spunk, then kissed her forehead. "Thank you."

Her eyes met his in shared understanding. "This wasn't a solo project."

"Maybe not. But you've given me so much — a true family, Ricky, another new son."

She glanced at the baby, who rested against her chest. "Little Todd Mallory?"

His throat tightened. "You really want to name him after my brother?"

Cindy's eyes were soft, her smile bright.

"Can you think of anything more fitting? This way we can embrace the good of our pasts." The baby's tiny fingers clutched hers. "And in him we have the promise of a whole new future."

Flynn stared at her, scarcely able to believe that he had captured this truly mercurial comet, that she was his wife, his love. For a moment he closed his eyes and uttered a now-familiar prayer of thanks.

Then she glanced up again, her bright green eyes so filled with life it made him ache.

Flynn smoothed the back of his hand over her cheek. "I didn't know it was possible for my love to grow each and every day."

Tenderness filled her expression. "We've been given a new beginning, the rarest of gifts."

Their hands clasped together, the pain of the past fading, the joy of tomorrow growing. Just as it had since they'd married a month after he proposed.

Knowing that the feelings they shared were a blessing directly from heaven, their eyes met. In that moment they left the past behind for good, looking to a future filled with hope, buoyed by love . . . and forever awash in the brilliant light of two hearts joined as one.

Dear Reader,

There are few things more heartrending than love denied. Especially when that love is impossibly out of reach. For Cindy Thompson, a woman of incredible spirit and equally strong faith, it is a road she would never have chosen to travel.

Which is why I was compelled to tell her story, to give voice to these characters who found a place in my heart, as well. I hope they will tread on yours, as they undertake their journey of both love and faith. And in the twining, discover that nothing is more important and binding than the ties of family.

God Bless.

Bonnie K. Winn

About the Author

†

A hopeless romantic, Bonnie K. Winn naturally turned to romance writing. This seasoned author of historical and contemporary romance has won numerous awards, including having been voted one of the Top Ten Romance Authors in America, according to *Affaire de Coeur*. Living in the foothills of the Rockies gives Bonnie plenty of inspiration and a touch of whimsy, as well. She shares her life with her husband, son and a spunky Westie terrier. Bonnie welcomes mail from her readers. You can write to her c/o Steeple Hill Books, 300 E. 42nd St., New York, NY 10017.

The employees of Thorndike Press hope you have enjoyed this Large Print book. All our Thorndike and Wheeler Large Print titles are designed for easy reading, and all our books are made to last. Other Thorndike Press Large Print books are available at your library, through selected bookstores, or directly from us.

For information about titles, please call:

(800) 223-1244

or visit our Web site at:

www.gale.com/thorndike
www.gale.com/wheeler

To share your comments, please write:

Publisher
Thorndike Press
295 Kennedy Memorial Drive
Waterville, ME 04901

Goshen County Library
2001 East "A" Street
Torrington, WY 82240
83-109